The Oath

Tales from a Revolution: Georgia

Also by Lars D. H. Hedbor,
available from Brief Candle Press:

The Prize: Tales From a Revolution - Vermont
The Light: Tales From a Revolution - New-Jersey
The Smoke: Tales From a Revolution - New-York
The Declaration: Tales From a Revolution - South-Carolina
The Break: Tales From a Revolution - Nova-Scotia
The Wind: Tales From a Revolution - West-Florida
The Darkness: Tales From a Revolution - Maine
The Path: Tales From a Revolution - Rhode-Island
The Freedman: Tales From a Revolution - North-Carolina
The Tree: Tales From a Revolution - New-Hampshire
The Mine: Tales From a Revolution - Connecticut
The Siege: Tales From a Revolution - Virginia
The Will: Tales From a Revolution - Pennsylvania
The Convention: Tales From a Revolution - Massachusetts
The Powder: Tales From a Revolution - Bermuda

The Oath

Lars D. H. Hedbor

Brief Candle
Press

Cover and book design: Brief Candle Press.
Cover image based on "California Spring," Albert Bierstadt, 1875. Courtesy of the Fine Arts Museums of San Francisco.
Map reproduction courtesy of Library of Congress, Geography and Map Division.
Fonts: Allegheney, Doves Type, and IM FELL English.

First Brief Candle Press edition published 2022.
www.briefcandlepress.com

ISBN: 978-1-942319-73-3

Dedication

*To the long-suffering
citizens of Haiti, who
deserve better than history
has granted them.*

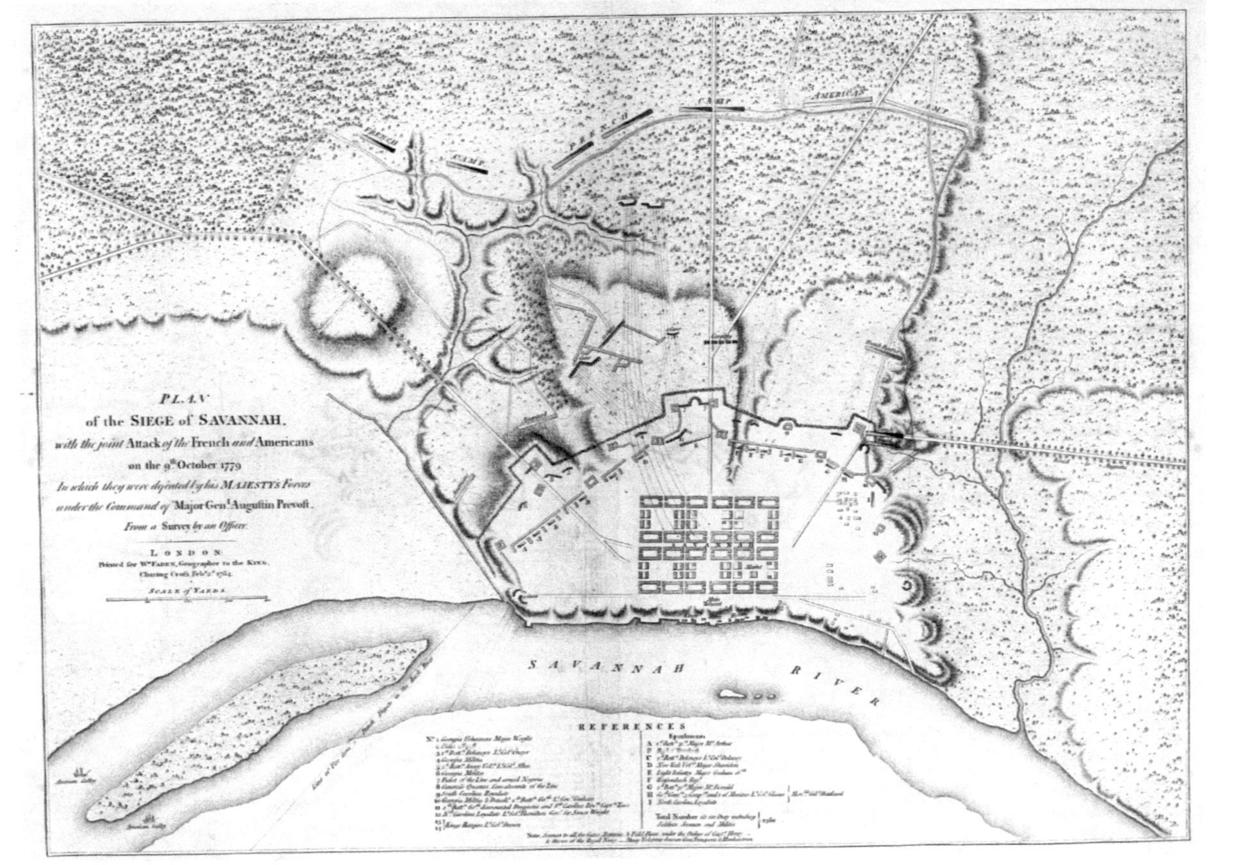

FRENCH CAMP
FRENCH CAMP
AMERICANS CAMP
PLAN
of the SIEGE of SAVANNAH.
with the joint Attack of the French and Americans
on the 9th October 1779
In which they were depicted by his MAJESTY's Forces
under the Command of Major Genl Augustin Prevost.
From a Survey by an Officer.
LONDON
Printed for Wm Faden, Geographer to the King,
Charing Cross, Feby 2d 1784.
SCALE of YARDS.
SAVANNAH RIVER
REFERENCES

Chapter I

The scratching of the court official's pen irritated James Hatch, but then, there wasn't much these days that didn't. It seemed to him that the man was taking entirely too much pleasure in shaping his elegant, proper copperplate letters across the page, in contrast to the limits of James' own untidy scrawl.

The man paused and read back to him. "Declaration of James Hatch to obtain the benefit of an Act of Congress passed June of 1832. State of Georgia, Walton County, on this Eleventh day of November, Eighteen hundred and thirty-three, personally appeared before the Superior Court of said County and State James Hatch, a resident of Walton County and the State aforesaid, aged seventy-four years, who being duly sworn according to law doth on his Oath make the following declaration in order to obtain the benefit of the provisions made by the Act of Congress passed June 7th, 1832."

The official looked up at James, the light from the window glinting off his glasses. "Right so far?"

"Aye, I reckon you've got my age and name right, and where I live. The rest, about the Congress, and the dates, I'll just have to trust that you know well enough."

It rankled him to have to come, hat in hand, to ask payment for service that took place a lifetime ago. More than that, though, he was not looking forward to the necessity of sharing the details of that service with this dandy, whose bravest act in this life had probably been to embrace the use of a steel nib for his pen over the old-fashioned quill.

Still, James reminded himself that his need was keen, and his cause was worthy. The money promised by Congress would enable him to make a real difference. He could swallow his pride for a chance to end the injustice around him.

Oblivious to James' unhappiness, the official said, "Now, can you tell me how and when you came to enlist in the Army?"

"Naturally. I am aged, but not yet daft. I joined up early in the year '79 — February, I think it was — and I heard that Captain Tolliver was raising a company of Virginians that would come to serve under Colonel Parker..."

◐◑

A cold gust blew in from the direction of the fallow tobacco fields, and James shifted uncomfortably, trying to hide the shiver that ran down his spine. The officer who stood haranguing the crowd before the tavern caught his movement, and glanced over at him with a quick flash of a smile on his face.

"You there, are you willing to serve to defend your country against the violence that the King sends hither? Will you stay here and wait in the chill of winter for the redcoats to put all to the torch and warm you thus? Or will you turn out and send them back to England whence they came?"

James did not much care for being personally singled out in this manner, but he could not dispute the appeal of the officer's call to duty. Although the past four years of warfare had little touched Virginia since independence had been declared, the newspapers and tavern talk were full of the suffering of New-England and warnings of the risk to the local ports and cities.

The officer wasn't finished, though. "I carry word that King George's troops have taken the port of Savannah, in Georgia, and that they mean to use that foothold to drive northward — all the way to Boston if they can — right over the ground where you have been trying to survive."

He looked each man before him in the eye to ensure that he had their full attention, and then waved an arm out toward the acres of tobacco stubble. "Would you see these fields run red with the blood of your neighbors? Will you stand by while the British seize your hard-won land and hand it over to some officer in their army to reward him for returning these states to the Crown's despotism? Will you leave it to some other man to defend your wives, your mothers, and your children from the perils of war?"

James' neighbor Phineas spoke up, answering in a deep rumble, "No, sir, I will not." He was joined by a ragged chorus of shouts and James found himself adding to it, without conscious volition.

"Or will you fight for our liberty, for our sacred honor, for our very way of life?"

This time, the answer was more unified, and James felt more committed to the loud cry, "Yes!" that he shouted with the other men.

It really was only a matter of doing what he owed to these friends and neighbors, never mind to his own family.

His father was too old to serve, and his brother far too young. His sisters both had newborn children to tend, and while James didn't know whether their husbands would heed the call to service, neither of them had turned out to hear the Virginian officer speak . . . So it was left to him to step up.

In short order, the captain was adding his name to the roster, asking briskly, "Have you a gun of your own, Private Hatch?"

James was forced to confess that he did not, and the officer dismissed his shamefaced explanations with a wave of his hand. "Never you mind, we'll get you equipped. Go and get your affairs in order, and I'll see you back here at sunrise. We'll muster and march out then for training."

He wasn't sure what he had expected his parents to think of his decision to enlist. His mother had only gasped and retreated to her bedroom, while his father had chewed at the side of his cheek for a long time before saying only, "I must see to your mother. Mind that you give her no cause for grief, son, while do what you feel your duty is."

James could almost see his father grow smaller as he added, "I do wish that you had come and sought my counsel before you rushed into this, James. You're a good boy, but I wonder if you know your own mind yet."

James did not answer, and the older man turned and left without waiting for him to do so. He wasn't sure what he would have said, even if the man had given him the opportunity. He was, after all, a man grown, and it rubbed him raw to be treated as though he were still a boy.

James was left feeling a sense of unfinished business when he departed the following morning, seen off only by the elderly slave who tended the kitchen hearth. His mother and brother were still abed, and his father had departed even earlier than James himself was up, on some business at a neighboring plantation.

Phineas was at least a friendly face in the small crowd that gathered in the dim morning chill, and James related to him the bewildering reception he'd gotten from his parents.

Phineas shrugged. "Your pa has never been much more than half-warm in his support for independence, James. I've heard that his kinfolk are on the other side, and he may just be worried that you will come to face your own blood in this war."

James shushed his friend with an urgent motion of his hand, urging quietly, "You keep those rumors to yourself. My father has never said a single thing that could give any man reason to doubt his loyalty to these United States, and just because his cousins haven't sent word doesn't mean they're Tories. Stories like that can get a man an appointment with a vat of pitch and a sack of feathers."

Phineas nodded his acquiescence, raising his hands in a mollifying gesture. He answered just a quietly. "As you say, James. I'm just suggesting that your parents might not be so much disapproving of your choice to join up as they are about which side you've chosen."

No matter how he tried , James couldn't dismiss the thought that there might have been a kernel of truth in Phineas' comments. He chewed over the thought, hardly noticing the distance they covered marching behind Captain Tolliver, as their officer had introduced himself. James knew that the war for independence was grinding to an apparent impasse in the north, and the news of the British incursion to their south had set some pessimistic chins to wagging about the tavern.

Perhaps his father was only worried that James had joined a hopeless cause, committing himself to open disloyalty to a King who would soon enough again hold sway over this country. James could see the disadvantages, should that come to pass.

On the other hand, the only way to keep such a thing from happening was for enough good men to step forward. When Phineas had spoken up, it had seemed only sensible to add his own voice to the cause, but now that he was shuffling through the morning mist, James couldn't help but second-guess himself.

He could have hung back when the officer was taking down men's names the day before, and faded away into the afternoon. He could have left as Tolliver was still in the process of working the crowd up into what served as a patriotic fervor, leaving the others to be enthralled by the man's words. He could even have faced the officer, when it came time to add his name to the roll, and declined.

Nobody had forced him to stick around, or answer the call, or put down his name; he needed to admit to himself that he had had some reason for doing all of these things. Was it to prove to his father that he was, in fact, a grown man, and not merely an apprentice planter on a tobacco plantation that might someday pass into his hands? Was it to prove to himself that he was capable of making a decision and standing by it?

Or had he merely allowed himself to be carried along by the moment, swept into a rushed choice to do what his friends and neighbors seemed to expect of him, without having taken the time to sufficiently consider the implications and consequences?

Regardless, he was committed now. Every step carried him further away from his home, and closer to an unknowable future. He had heard enough reports of the battles in New-England to know that the British forces were not a threat to be taken lightly. Nor were the hazards of disease and injury even without the action of the enemy to be ignored.

The enemy! What a thing to call men who included not only the British soldiers who had come across the ocean to suppress American intransigence, but those loyal subjects from the communities around James' home who now stood beside the redcoats.

He might have played childhood games with them as a boy, might even share blood with them, and now he must confront the very real possibility that a familiar face might appear at the far end of his musket.

Worse, a choice would have to be made; who would pull their trigger first?

As the recruits marched on into the morning, James thought about the boys he'd known who had become scarce as the fervor for independence had grown into an unstoppable thing. Frederick Kilburne, for one. His father had been a crown official of one sort or another, though James had never bothered himself to find out more. Once it became a matter of greater interest, the Kilburne family had already left for friendlier parts.

William Huntsman he was quite sure of, as well. James had heard him in a heated discussion at the tavern one night, defending the honor of the British army defeated at Saratoga. He was arguing that the Americans had no right to continue to hold them prisoner, when the condition of their surrender had been that they'd be shipped back to England.

This was while the captives were still up at Cambridge, in New-England. It was an irony that long after William had taken his musket and angry words to the British line, the army he had insisted ought to have been sent home was newly installed in a camp right here in Virginia. James hoped not to come within range of his musket — William was known for his ability to load and fire as quickly as any man in all the district.

For that matter, James prayed that, when the time came for him to line up on some field of battle, there would be no man on the opposite side whose face was even slightly familiar.

He glimpsed a great truth of warfare in that moment, before his first day of training had even begun. It is easier to strive for the death and misfortune of men who are unknown to you than to consider bringing harm to someone whose humanity you knew at close range.

Of course, once his training commenced, there were far more practical truths to grapple with. James had fired a musket many times before, naturally, but it was something yet again to learn how to fire one in time with one's fellow soldiers. Speed was still of the essence — troops that could fire three times in a minute self-evidently stood a greater chance of striking their enemy than those who could barely manage one ragged round in a minute's time.

Too, there were the details of marching in a well-spaced formation, instead of stumbling along bunched up in a clump that made a handy target for an enemy artillery company. And there were many, many lessons that were not delivered formally, but through experience alone.

Choosing a dry place for a tent, so that you wouldn't wake up with a rivulet flooding over your feet, building a proper fire with a minimum of smoke to avoid alerting British scouts — or worse, their Indian allies! — to your presence, and feeding yourself on scarcely half of a legal ration were all critical lessons to learn, but which appeared in no manual of drill.

It wasn't only rations that were short, either. When James had joined up, the captain had promised that all recruits would be clothed in a stoutly-made uniform and equipped with a well-founded musket. Instead, each man had been issued some indifferent scraps of cloth that might be charitably called breeches, no shoes save what they had come with, and no better than one musket for every three men.

There were always promises that another shipment would come any day now, as promised by the distant Congress, but James remembered the advice his father had given him in a very different context. It applied well here, too.

"Spend no promise until it lies in your purse. No matter how well a man means his word, the true value of his intent cannot be properly judged until he has followed through on it."

The circumstance that had occasioned this particular lesson had been the failure of a childhood friend to repay a loan, which had left James short of the price of a horse that he had yearned for. Another man was prepared to buy up the mare while James scrambled to get together the necessary funds, so he had gone to his father to ask for assistance.

After delivering his words of wisdom, his father had dug the money James needed out of his own purse — and hadn't even said anything when not a month later the horse had stepped into a foxhole and broken its leg. The loss of both the horse and the friend who owed him money had clearly been lesson enough for his father's purposes.

James had remembered his anger at the unpaid debt, though, and had diligently repaid his father for the loan, even though he had gotten little material benefit from it.

In any event, as dearly as he had wanted to enjoy the use of the horse, the lesson he'd learned from the incident had been of even greater value. So James wasn't left with nothing at all to eat when promised rations were delayed. He'd held back some of his biscuit and salt beef where others had eaten what they had, relying upon resupply before the next meal.

As for the guns, that promised to be a more serious issue, if the company were ordered into action before that deficiency could be remedied. As it was, the squads were training in shifts, handing off what guns they did have from one man to the next as they took turns in drill.

Even with that expedient, they were but pantomiming the loading and firing sequence, as all available powder and balls were being conserved for men facing real enemies instead of wooden forms at the far end of the drill ground.

Then came the day when a supply train arrived and suddenly, there were muskets enough for every man, along with more powder and shot than they could readily carry. The men mustered out in proper uniforms, and if they still had to wear their own shoes, it was of little import, as everything else was finally available in ample quantity.

They stood in their ranks to listen to Captain Tolliver explain the abrupt shower of the very things that they'd been so desperate to lay their hands on for so long. Listening to him, James swallowed hard and tried not to let his reaction show outwardly.

Drill was over, and it the company had its orders to march for battle.

Chapter 2

The court official's pen had fallen silent, and he peered over his glasses at James. "Your training concluded, you marched thence to...?"

James started slightly, having been lost in memory for a moment. "Ah, what a march it was, too. Clear across Virginia, all the way through North-Carolina, *and* South-Carolina, and we didn't stop until we reached Georgia, where the accursed redcoats had taken Savannah. We were meant to besiege that city, and with the assistance of the French, take it back."

"So you marched to Savannah directly from the training ground? Do you remember the names of any men who were with you there, whose testimonies will lend weight to your own, should it come into question?"

James bristled. "For what cause might my testimony be brought into question, young man? Do you doubt that I served exactly as I've said?"

The other man took off his glasses and wiped them with his neckerchief in a nervous gesture. "Not at all. You've given your oath, and I have no cause whatever to doubt anything you've said under that oath. Those whom the Congress has charged with verifying the accounts used to qualify men for the past pension acts have found that such details make the job far easier than is otherwise the case."

He put his glasses back on and fixed James with a steady gaze. "If you recall men with whom you served, all the better, but if not, I have no reason to doubt that you will be found to qualify for your pension."

James relaxed, his features settling into a sad frown of recollection. "Aye, there were men whose names I can recall as easily as I do the names of my own sons." He leaned forward in his seat. "Bravest man I ever met was at Savannah, one of those Frenchmen. Fellow by the name of Claude Legrand, came up from Saint-Domingue as a volunteer..."

●◯●

Footsore and weary beyond any measure he could have previously named, James and his company came around a bend in the road, to a place where the ever-present canopy of trees opened up to the first broad vista he'd seen since they'd left Augusta.

He immediately noticed the veritable forest of masts upon the water before the city. The man next to him remarked under his breath, "It's as they said — the French acted as though this were their fight alone, and not ours against the invaders. They've laid siege to the town without waiting for our arrival."

James shrugged. Matters of strategy and political wrangling within the alliance were of little interest to him. He was just glad that they weren't coming to this fight without any aid at all.

He turned his gaze away from the ships and toward the town they menaced. Most of what he could see from the road were the redoubts, still consisting of raw earth, belying their hasty and recent construction. The maws of the British batteries of cannon could just be perceived through their narrow slits in the breastworks.

Gazing at the black depths of those bores, visible as little more than dots from this distance, James was glad that they were still dark, and not belching flame and death in their direction. The terrain was too flat to make out anything beyond the British emplacements, but as the company proceeded on the road that was built up through the marshy approach to the city, French scouts met the head of the column.

After a hasty conference, the American troops were led on to a road that skirted the British guns at what James fervently hoped was a safe remove. Soon enough, they were being welcomed into a camp consisting of crisp, clean tents, set up in good order, as if the French forces were simply enjoying an outing in the countryside.

James was all too conscious that their own tents were comparatively worn and dirty as the company labored to get them set up before darkness fell. He found himself taking extra care to set the pegs firmly into the ground, and wishing that the company were as disciplined as their hosts outside the town in laying out the placement of their tents.

Before too long, a rank of French soldiers approached the growing American encampment, and James' sergeant was called over to meet them. James was surprised to note that the French troops were all Negroes of one shade or another, although they were dressed little differently from the rest of the French forces.

His sergeant returned with three of the newcomers, introducing them. "Our friends have sent some of their number over to aid us in getting ourselves established here. Do any of you lot speak any of the French?"

James' squad looked around at each other, mute in answer. The man shook his head, saying, "'Tis a pity, as only Thomas here has any English."

Thomas grinned at the mention of his name. "It is not a problem, Sergeant. I introduce ourselves." James found the man's accent unfamiliar and heavy, but he could understand what he was saying readily enough.

He squared his shoulders, pointing first at his own chest. "I am Thomas Lambert, of the *Chasseurs-Volontaires* from Saint-Domingue." James noticed that he pronounced his own name differently than the sergeant had — it sounded more like "toe-mah" — but before he could untangle the rest of the man's introduction, he was already pointing to the tall man beside him.

"This is Claude Legrand. His name is easy for remember — he is *grand*, tall, hmm?" Thomas grinned broadly again at his own witticism, but James only really grasped that the tall man was named Claude, and then his attention was on the final member of the trio.

"He is Henri LeBon, and name is good for him, too. He is good man, good name." Thomas clapped his hands together and looked around the growing encampment. "We will help you now. Need hearths, fires built, yes? Perhaps some earthworks, hmm?"

The sergeant stepped forward once again. "That would be a great service, yes. Justin, go and fetch some shovels from the supply cart for these men, and get enough for four other men to work with them."

When the private had returned with the tools, the sergeant and Thomas engaged in a brief, but good-natured argument over where the work ought to be done. James found himself rounded up to join the French soldiers in their digging, along with three other members of the squad.

Thomas seemed to have taken it upon himself to encourage

his fellow Frenchmen, shouting cheerful exhortations to them in their own language. James wished he could understand what was being said, if only to be able to join in what was clearly happy banter among them.

Under their shovels, a field hearth was quickly roughed out, and then they turned to the heavier labor of building up a trench in front of the American positions. James noticed that the soil here was sandier than what he was accustomed to which made it relatively easy to heap up in front of the trench. But when they hit an area of heavy clay, the work slowed down considerably, until Henri came over and pointed to where the earth was sandier again just a bit uphill from where they were digging.

By the time it was dark enough that they could no longer work effectively, they'd built up a berm that would at least permit a few men to find shelter behind it, should the British come out of the town to raise a ruckus.

As they'd worked, James had developed a sense of each of the French men who'd been sent to help them. Thomas remained ebullient even as the afternoon wore on. Though James' own shoulders were screaming for relief from the unceasing motion of driving his shovel into the ground, breaking free the clump of soil and tossing it onto the growing berm, Thomas was always ready with a smile and an encouraging comment.

Henri seemed to know the most about what was needed to build up the earthworks to protect the American positions, as he and Thomas conferred regularly before Thomas came back to point out one detail or another about working with the different types of soil they encountered.

Claude was the quiet one of the group, nowhere near as free

with a smile as was Thomas. And when one of the other American soldiers accidentally sent a clod of earth astray from his shovel, and it struck Claude in the leg, the man's smile disappeared entirely, and he whirled to confront the digger.

Thomas came over to intercede, his tone calming even before he'd learned all the details from both men. Patrick, the American swore that it had been a pure accident, and offered apologies for his clumsiness.

Claude frowned grimly as Thomas relayed Patrick's statement. He made a couple of comments, bitter in tone, and motioned to the other end of the line, where more of the group was working.

Thomas turned to Patrick and said, gravely, "My friend LeGrand is upset before by order from our general that we *Chasseurs-Volontaires* must work only on trenches. We came to be soldiers, not just dig." He shrugged broadly, raising his hands. "Who am I to say what work we do? Still, it would make happier if you help Henri at *that* end, hmm?"

Claude stood with his arms crossed, his mouth compressed in a tight line. Patrick raised his own hands in a gesture of acceptance, and nodded. "If it will make him happy, I don't mind. It were an accident, but I don't blame him for being sore over having to work at this on our account."

Patrick took his shovel and trudged down to where Henri was working, and Thomas called out to his countryman, explaining the change. Henri nodded and shot a significant look in Claude's direction.

James found that his sympathies were with Claude. After all, it was bad enough to be told that your skills were only good enough to perform heavy labor, but to be pelted with a heavy clump of soil in the bargain would have shortened any man's temper to the breaking point.

He didn't know Patrick well, and had no reason to doubt the sincerity of his explanation or of his apology — but he was glad that Thomas had interceded.

The stormy expression on Claude's face finally settled down to no more than a frown in the direction of Patrick's retreating form, and he picked up his own shovel from where he'd dropped it.

James stepped into Patrick's position, taking great care not to repeat the other man's mistake, and made it a point to smile encouragingly at Claude from time to time as the man worked beside him. They continued without further incident until it was time to quit for the night.

After the French had returned to their tents and the Americans were taking their ease around the new firepit, Patrick appeared suddenly beside James and spoke with quiet menace. "Was you backing up that blackbird when he was griping about that little bit of dirt on his leg?"

James was taken aback by the hostility in the other man's tone. "I thought that was an accident, Patrick."

The other man spat into the fire, raising a hiss that seemed almost as malevolent as his expression. "It were an accident, but it were no big deal, either, until he made it into one. I've got my eye on you, Hatch. You need to stick together with your own kind, when there's any kind of trouble."

James glowered at the other man. "Those Frenchmen were come to help us with work that they could just as easily have left us to do on their own. I thought it better to be grateful for their help than to treat them as no more than servants."

Patrick uttered a harsh bark of laughter. "Just because the French let them blackbirds put on airs and act as though they were just the same as us doesn't mean that they ain't blackbirds. They're good for one thing — work — and they only understand one language — the lash. You might be impressed that they speak the French in some fashion, but at least I know what they are."

James felt his jaw sag in disbelief at the other man's words. While he hadn't met many free Negroes in Virginia, he'd known them to be skilled tradesmen and had from time to time seen his father hire one for some sort of work or another around the plantation.

He was glad enough for their appearance here when it developed that they'd been sent to help with the heavy work of setting up camp. There was no doubt in his mind that without Henri's knowledge of where the pockets of clay were hidden under the surface, their progress would have been much impeded.

Finally, he answered Patrick slowly. "I believe in being grateful for help, and in not biting a hand extended in friendly assistance, no matter what sort of man it might belong to."

Patrick shook his head, evidently disgusted at James' response. "It'll be your own hand that gets bit, if you keep hanging out with animals," he said, turning away. "Mind you learn the difference before it's too late to save yourself that nip."

Chapter 3

Sieges, James had expected, were primarily exercises in boredom. Once they were properly encamped — "invested," as the lieutenant liked to say — there would be little to do, outside of the regular drill and the incessant mending of clothes and tents, and repairing weaponry that had become worn from use and age.

Now he *wished* that sieges were so dull a time.

The day had started plainly enough, with a return to the earthworks, and Thomas' enthusiasm helping bring some relief from the hard manual labor. James' shoulders were already sore from the prior day's exertions, and they screamed anew at the fresh demands he placed on them with the shovel.

Patrick kept his distance, and though he greeted the French soldiers politely when they arrived during breakfast, James could not forget the bitter words the other man had spat the night before. He noticed, too, the coolness with which Patrick addressed Thomas, and wondered whether that were new since the confrontation with Claude, or if he just hadn't noticed the man's attitude before now.

Fortunately, the sheer competence of the French, and their constant heavy effort, made it nearly impossible for the Americans to find cause for any ill feelings, save perhaps a kernel of resentment at having to work hard enough to keep up.

The British could be seen atop their breastworks, observing

the newly arrived American forces, and more than once, James wondered when they would open fire and test the trenches he was helping to construct.

That evening, he got his answer. Before dark, a crack like a thunderclap sounded from the British line, and some sentry howled out, "Take cover!" James' squad threw themselves behind the berm, and James found himself making an urgent appeal to the great Author of the world as he waited for the shot to find ground.

Beside him, Henri was sitting relaxed with his back against the berm, and past Henri, James was amazed to see Claude staring at the British line, his hands on his hips, and an appraising expression on his face as he followed the path of an incoming cannon ball with his eyes.

James could not see over the berm to watch along with the Frenchman, but Claude's grim smile told him the shot had fallen short, and was no threat to the American line yet. Claude noticed him staring, and said something in an amused tone, motioning up past the berm.

Beside him, Henri called back in French, and casually got to his feet, brushing the clinging soil from his breeches. He held out a hand to help James to his feet, but James waved him off with a smile and stood up on his own.

Claude caught his eye and pointed out at the open ground before the American trenches. James spotted the cannon ball lying in the dirt an easy hundred paces away, and the ugly scar in the soil behind where it had come to rest.

His sergeant approached from behind him. "They're still trying to get their range. Fortunately, if our French friends are correct, they have no guns that can reach us here." He glanced down at where the other members of the squad were slowly getting up and recovering their tools. "Still, good practice to get behind cover until the shot has spent itself."

He glanced over at Claude and shook his head. "No need to be a hero like that fool. We can ill afford to lose any man on this line, even if we do have the British over there outnumbered and surrounded." The sergeant walked back toward the first line of tents, still shaking his head.

James didn't think that Claude was being foolish, or even trying to be a hero. There was genuine value in observing the British gunnery, so long as one could watch the shot coming in and arrange to be somewhere else if it seemed to be aimed true.

If the sergeant was correct, they were outside of danger of being struck by round shot, and they were well out of range of grapeshot. It would take a lucky bounce of a cannon ball to do any harm — but stranger things had happened on battlefields, so James supposed that Claude's insouciance really was a bad idea.

Thomas approached Claude then, and they shared a laughing conversation, punctuated by Claude mimicking the path of the spent ball with his hand. He indicated its final resting place with a rude mouth noise, and both men laughed again.

Thomas spied James observing them and called out, "They British fellows been firing cannon at us for many days." He shrugged in what James now recognized as his typical broad gesture. "Let them waste powder and ball. We have work to do, hmm?" James nodded and bent to pick up his shovel.

At the end of the day, while he sat in the gathering darkness with his company grimly spooning down the thin gruel that passed for supper, James was puzzled to hear a sudden buzzing sound behind his head, followed by the crack of a musket shot from the direction of the berm.

Someone else shouted an alarm, and pandemonium erupted as every man threw down whatever he was doing and rushed to lay hands on a gun — any gun — and return fire. The sentries discharged their weapons into the darkness, the flashes from their muzzles blinding James for a moment.

He finally reached his tent and was relieved to see that his own musket was still there. He gathered it and his cartridge bag and ran back outside, but the excitement was already over. No further fire was coming from the British side, and James' sergeant was urging men to lower their shouldered weapons.

"You're more likely to shoot one of our own than to actually hit a redcoat now. They sent a party out to harry us, and having done that, beat a retreat back to their fortifications. Now you all are rewarding their effort — why, just look at how they have us all stirred up. and at the cost of just a couple of rounds of musket fire from a handful of men."

Not wishing to earn the man's ire, James slung his musket and buttoned up his cartridge bag, turning to go back to his tent. Sheepishly, the other men in the encampment followed suit, but nobody was going to sleep soundly that night, especially after one man found a ball had gone right through his tent just where his head would have lain, had he been on his bedroll.

A few nights later, as the troops were settling down into regular, dull siege operations, it happened again. This time, a volley of shots came from the direction of the Americans' right, and again, everyone in the camp scrambled for their weapons.

They were better prepared to engage with the enemy now,

and the sides exchanged several volleys. The British seemed to have flanked the American camp, though, and their fire was more sustained and concentrated than it had been in the first incident.

This time, some of the shots found their marks. James heard one man nearby him cry out and fall to the ground with a dreadful, loose thud. Everyone dropped as low as they could at a barked order from the lieutenant, and they continued firing in the direction of the shots they could hear in the darkness.

In what seemed like some sort of slow-motion nightmare, James repeated the motions of loading, priming, aiming, and firing his musket over and over again. Not once did he lay eyes on a redcoat, instead basing his aim on wherever he perceived a shot from the other side to have originated.

He heard someone roaring orders in French from the next camp over, and supposed that they, too, had come under fire. He knew that Thomas' regiment was well over on the far side of the line, and wondered for a brief moment how they were faring.

However, there was little time to ponder such matters in the urgent rush to continue the fight right here. There was no coordinated firing sequence such as they'd been drilled on; instead, every man was firing at will, right up to the moment when he heard the captain start to shout himself hoarse, "Cease fire! Stop! No more, curse you! The British have tricked us into firing on each other!"

The awful truth of what the officer had said took only a moment to penetrate the chaotic thoughts that roiled through James' mind. This pitched battle had been between not allied troops and a British incursion in force, but the American and French regiments?

James shifted in a flash from hoping that every one of his shots had found its target, to praying for his own inaccuracy and the good fortune to have missed anything vital with each and every volley.

The thought that French soldiers, who had joined in this war in order to help America gain its independence from Britain, might even now be groaning their last at his hands made James' blood run cold, and as he slung his musket over his shoulder, he felt his gorge rising at the repercussions that this incident might have.

Would the French abandon the siege entirely, leaving the Americans to either try to press forward or to slink away, abandoning this town to the hands of the enemy? Would they seek some other form of retribution, demanding courts-martial and punishments for all involved? Just how awful would the consequences be for the mayhem that the British had successfully sown between the allies?

For once, James was grateful that he was no more than a private soldier, and that he did not have to answer for these sorts of questions. It was just possible, of course, that the only losses had been in the American camp, and that the French could put this whole thing down to British mischief-making.

By the following morning, it was clear that men had been lost in both camps, but none of the dire consequences James feared came to pass. He felt a sense of relief when Thomas came bounding into the camp around midmorning, his usual grin held in abeyance until he'd assured himself that all of the Americans he knew had been spared in the night's action.

After checking in on James, Thomas grimaced, "Those British fellows have made many tricks since we arrived here. We are unfortunate in our enemies this day, I think." That much,

James could agree with wholeheartedly. Thomas clapped him on the back and finished, "I must return to camp for to eat, but we will see you soon, hmm?"

James nodded, and watched the Frenchman stride back in the direction of his camp.

There had been little enough opportunity to get to know their allies better. Between the language barrier and the demands of their strenuous work, they didn't talk about anything that wasn't directly related to the tasks at hand. He wondered, though, what would have induced someone like Thomas, or Henri, or Claude to leave their homes and come to fight in a war that wasn't their own.

He vaguely grasped that the main French army was here on the orders of their king, who was motivated to make trouble for the English wherever possible in the world. Old grudges died hard, and he'd heard his father comment that the French loss of Quebec was ever fresh in the minds of the political and military leaders at Versailles.

But what had driven the men from Saint-Domingue to join in the martial aims of the distant court in France?

He wondered for a moment whether their condition was as wretched as that of many of the freed slaves he'd encountered, but rejected that possibility quickly. The sunny disposition of Thomas, the quiet assurance of Henri, or the confident boldness of Claude were all impossible to imagine of people who were maintained in the low social position of the freedmen he'd known in Virginia.

Whatever their motivation, he was glad that they had chosen to overlook Patrick's barbs, and were willing to share their hard-won knowledge of the terrain and the disposition of the enemy — and most of all, their hard work.

Today, it was going to be time to repay the favor, as most of James' company would be joining a crew of French soldiers — though not Thomas' — in extending a trench closer to the British fortifications. The plan, as James' sergeant had explained it, was to make it possible to get within musket range of the British defenders. What would happen after that was left unsaid . . . but James doubted that they would be enduring very many dull days once these trenches were completed.

Chapter 4

The trench work was proceeding at a good clip, though the crews were slowed somewhat by the necessity of staying quiet, lest the British be alerted to the plan. James' arms and shoulders were past exhaustion now, and he maintained the repetitive motions of digging, lifting, and throwing soil primarily by a force of will.

As they were working more closely to the British lines now, a guard was posted to defend them, should they come under attack. Thomas' company had been assigned this duty, and James found himself envying them as they strode back and forth, guns at the ready, eyes alert in the direction of the British fortifications.

The line of earthworks surrounding the town were obscured from this range, though, by a tangle of trees and brush — which the sergeant called an "abattis" — that the defenders had thrown about to provide themselves with cover. Later, James would guess that this was how the British had surprised them.

He heard shouting before any shots this time, as the French raised the alarm, and he looked up to see a force of what had to be hundreds of British soldiers boiling out from a gap in the abattis. The first volley of musketry from the French soldiers seemed to barely slow them down as they rushed out and formed up to march on the trench where he stood.

"Move, move, get back and let the guard engage them!"

James wasn't even certain who had shouted the command, but he was happy enough to follow it. The first balls from the British fire were starting to *thunk* into the back of the trench, making this a decidedly unwelcoming place to stay.

As he joined the rest of the unarmed laborers in rushing toward the relative safety of the encampments, James saw Thomas, his expression serious and focused, tearing open the end of a cartridge with his teeth as he loaded his musket. The French soldier met his gaze and motioned with his chin for James to hurry, flashing a quick smile to him before his attention returned to the gun he was working.

Back at the encampment, the work party wasted no time in arming themselves, and James dashed with his fellow soldiers back toward the fracas as soon as he had his gun, tightening the straps of the cartridge bag as he ran.

It appeared that the British were falling back, as more French and American forces rushed forward to engage them, but it was tough to get a clear idea of exactly what was happening in the growing cloud of choking, gray gun smoke that drifted up from where the warmest action was centered.

His lieutenant shouted for the company to form up in a proper line and prepare to present a volley. The routine of loading and firing, drilled any number of hundreds of times, took over and James could hardly remember later the details of the actual skirmish. He was aware only of the commands now shouted and echoed down the line, and the grim, deadly work of the firing sequence.

The routine was interrupted by the cry of a man struck by an enemy shot, but once the ranks had closed around the hole he left, the loading and firing sequence picked up where it had been stopped.

James was aware of when the line reached and clambered through the trench he had lately been engaged in digging, but only as a minor annoyance in the process of working their way toward the enemy.

Ahead of them, the French were exhorting one another to move forward. A breeze cleared away the smoke, and James could see the bayonets of the French line flashing now in the sunlight. By their excited cries and surge forward, he could tell when the British turned and ran for the safety of their redoubt.

The lieutenant called out for the American line to hang back — "Don't forget that they have cannon up there!" — but in the thrill of breaking the British line, the French apparently had no such caution.

They paid dearly for their error.

The first blast from the cannon sounded, deeper and louder than the musket fire that still crackled over the field. As his ears recovered, James could hear men screaming and commands being shouted in French, and he felt his gorge rise once again at the carnage that had been produced by that single shot.

Retreating wildly from the trap into which they had been lured, the French came back toward the American line at a run, and the lieutenant gave the command for his own forces to retreat, as well.

Another roar from the cannon behind them gave James' feet wings in his flight from the deadly threat. A French soldier, his white uniform splattered with crimson, ran past him, gasping and weeping. Suddenly disoriented, James cast about himself, unsure that he was even running in the right direction. It was then that the front of the trench rose up out of the swirling smoke before him, and he gratefully threw himself over it into relative safety behind the berm.

Down in the trench, a makeshift hospital had sprung up. Wounded soldiers were being helped, or carried, or dragged, and the sharp metallic tang of blood filled James' nose. A soldier who seemed to be unhurt shouted something at James, and motioned him over with an urgent wave of his arm.

A man on the ground before him screamed in agony as the first soldier shouted unintelligible instructions at James, who shook his head to indicate his incomprehension. The soldier then grabbed his hand and pantomimed holding pressure on the wounded man's leg, where blood surged out of a ragged hole in his flesh onto the fresh soil of the makeshift shelter.

James followed the instructions as well as he could, while the soldier worked around him, tying on a strip of cloth above the wound and wrapping a piece of wood in it to form a tourniquet. Tightening it with determined motions and ignoring the cries of pain from the man on the ground, the first soldier muttered something in French, then brushed James' hands out of the way to assess whether he'd succeeded in stanching the flow of blood. A second later, he nodded briskly, seeming satisfied. He then stood and motioned for James to follow him to the next wounded man.

James could hear the injured soldier behind him moaning, over and over, "*Maman, maman, maman,*" and didn't need to speak any French at all to feel his heart lurch at the man's cries for his mother in his hour of desperate need.

The next patient — apparently shot through the chest with a musket ball — fell silent and limp even as the impromptu surgeon was still trying to gauge the severity of his injuries. The medic tried to rouse him for a moment, and then uttered what James could only guess was a curse before squeezing his eyes shut in an attempt to deny the tears that trickled from them.

The surgeon finally drew a deep, shuddering breath, and rose again, James trailing behind him, to look for someone he could help.

Further down the trench, a man lay alone on his side, one foot twitching fitfully, and as they approached, James gasped in horror to see Thomas, his face drawn tight in a rictus of pain.

He hurried to his friend's side, the surgeon saying something in an irritable tone behind him. Thomas' free hand was clutched to his side, and he was gasping for air, but James could see at a glance that his friend's efforts were hopeless. He knelt beside the mortally wounded man.

Thomas saw him and James thought his eyes flickered in recognition. The dying man's mouth twitched in an attempt at a smile, and he said faintly, "Those British fellows, they tricked us good this time, hmm?"

The energy spent speaking seemed to exhaust the last of the man's energy, and his eyes rolled back in his head. After a moment, James could see his chest rise as he inhaled sharply, and then he was still.

Chapter 5

eath was no stranger to a soldier. James had buried companions before, whether they had been stuck down by accidents, enemy fire, or just the age-old foe of all military forces, the waves of illness that would sweep through an encampment. However, seeing the last breath sigh out of a man who had just minutes before been full of lively purpose and unexplored plans, so that he was now reduced to just another broken corpse, was somehow more difficult to accept.

James forced himself upright, and turned away from Thomas, not even hearing the moans of the other wounded men around him, or the angry call of the surgeon. It felt as though everything around him were moving at an absurdly slow pace, and his own breath sounded harsh and ragged in his throat.

He started to stumble away, but the French surgeon — if he even was that — grabbed his arm and shouted something in his face. Shaking his head sharply, James heard himself raise his own voice in reply, "I can't. I just cannot. Let me go back to my company."

He tried to shake his arm free, but the Frenchman gripped it more tightly and shouted again, waving his free hand at the wounded men who still lay about them in the trench. Regaining his senses somewhat, James noticed that he and the Frenchman were the only two there who appeared to be unhurt, and he slowly grasped that the other man *needed* his aid. He chewed his lip for a moment, and then nodded, meeting the surgeon's eye.

"All right. Tell me what you need of me." The Frenchman's expression softened, and he said something in a more soothing tone, releasing James' arm and motioning to the next man who needed their help.

By the time the real surgeon arrived, James and the ersatz medic had moved the less-badly wounded to one end of the trench, and were starting to lift and remove the bodies of those who had died and bring them out for proper burial. James couldn't help but notice that the members of the *Chasseurs-Volontaires* made up a surprising proportion of the dead and most gravely wounded.

Again, he found himself wondering at the motivation that could have sparked such gallantry in the face of the enemy. Perhaps it was pride, then, or even a sense of duty to a king who had fostered a society where these men had been able to establish themselves. Or, he supposed, it could be that they were striving to prove themselves the equal of the regiments raised from France itself, by showing such bravery and eagerness to serve in this fight that none could dare to question their place in society.

James was struck by a thought that was both strange and chilling as he and the Frenchman positioned themselves at the head and feet of a man whose uniform was soaked through with blood as red as their own. These Negroes had proved themselves to be good soldiers, knowledgeable companions, and brave . . . *men*. Men no different from himself, save that he still breathed, and they had sacrificed themselves for the cause of American freedom.

His entire life up to this moment, he'd never questioned the order of things. Slaves were bought and sold like any farm animal, and distinguished themselves from horses and cattle primarily in the degree of mischief they could get into, if not adequately supervised. He'd always approved of seeing a man use a gentle hand with his slaves, just as he appreciated a man who could manage a team of oxen without too heavy a reliance on the whip.

Yet one did not grow overly sentimental about selling an extra foal in the fall, if the money would come in handy and the stables were full. Nor were the children of slaves kept around once they were mature enough to take up work in the fields, if there was not sufficient work to employ them all.

But seeing them as the children of men and women, whose capacity for love and heartbreak were as great as his own? Could that be reconciled with the fact that slaves recovered from such events as would break the spirit of any white man?

His practical side rebelled against the thought, even as he watched a puddle of blood spill from the chest of the Negro he was helping to move, demonstrating no difference whatever from the blood already spilled from the white man whose corpse waited beside him.

Everyone knew that Negroes lacked the more refined sensibilities, that they made crude and strange music, and ate a degraded and pitiful diet. Yet Thomas and his squad had made a point of returning to their own encampment for meals, after sampling the food that the American kettles offered.

Thomas had made comments about the declining quality of the foodstuffs available from French stores, and had been happy enough to try what the Americans were eating. Though he had feigned politeness, James had caught the Frenchman's look of revulsion at the plain mush he had sampled, before making excuses for them to go back and eat with their own regiment.

Who, then, had the more refined palate, and who was satisfied to eat a dull and coarse variety of porridges, occasionally relieved by a thin stew? The assumption that one group of men had more elevated tastes than the other did not stand up to even casual observation.

Too, James had never thought twice about the policy against educating slaves, accepting without a second thought the supposition that such education would be wasted on them. A wise man would not try to teach a pig to sing, nor would he try to teach a slave to ponder the higher qualities of philosophy or art. Yet who was he to cast aspersions on the intellectual capacities of a man who spoke both his native French and sufficient English to serve as a translator between his men and the Americans?

As he and the Frenchman returned to the trench for another torn and bloody set of remains, James was so absorbed by these difficult and unexpected thoughts that it took him a moment to realize that the surgeon was calling out to him in English.

"Should you not return to your unit, lest they presume you lost in the action?" The man's accent was nearly imperceptible, which startled James, but he recovered himself and answered.

"There are only two more dead to remove, and I do not want to leave just you and him to do it." He motioned to the other Frenchman with a tilt of his head.

"Ah, my assistant and I can manage, but if you believe you can be spared for another few minutes, I suppose that your help would be welcome enough." He turned to the other man and said something in rapid-fire French.

The surgeon's assistant answered him, and the surgeon nodded thoughtfully. "Alexandre tells me he thinks one of these men was known to you?"

James swallowed hard and pointed to where Thomas lay, "Aye, sir, that fellow was a part of the team sent to help us build up a berm before the American encampment. He spoke good English, and we had already become friends."

"I would be glad to spare you having to carry your friend out of here, if you like," the surgeon said, gently.

James thought for a moment and then shook his head. "I owe him this last service, sir. He died protecting those of us who were building these earthworks, including myself, so it seems only right that I should do what I can to help put him to rest."

The surgeon nodded. "It's a kindness, and a measure of respect that too few of these fellows get."

James looked at him sharply, wondering whether the arguments that had roiled in his mind had been so visible on his face that this man could read them so clearly. He did not get the chance to ask, though.

"When you are finished and go back to your troop, you may tell them that you were detained to assist Doctor Perrault."

James nodded, and the surgeon returned to the grisly work before him. He did not envy Perrault having to finish the job of removing limbs too damaged to save, stitching up wounds that would likely fester and kill in the end, and closing forever the eyes of those who he could not help at all.

He called out to the surgeon's assistant, heedless of the fact that the man could not understand his words, "Come, then, let us carry my friend out of here."

After carefully arranging Thomas' hands across his chest and sliding the lids shut over his friend's sightless eyes, James nodded to the other man, who was positioned at the dead soldier's feet.

Lifting Thomas up felt no different to him than had any of the other dead soldiers. A slack, dense weight, a chill in the flesh beneath his fingers, and the knowledge that yet another man had taken his last meal, his last aim, and his last breath.

After Thomas was laid gently beside the other bodies, the surgeon called out to his assistant, and the man departed at a trot for the French encampment. Perrault said to James, "I've sent him to get more men to help retrieve the dead and wounded from the field. We'll need a senior officer, as well, to persuade those British *salauds* to let us tend to our casualties."

He gestured back to where the American tents could just be seen. "Go, and take your rest. You've earned it. You may tell your commanding officer that those are the doctor's orders."

Back at camp, James made his way back toward his tent. Before he reached its sanctuary, though, his sergeant spotted him and approached.

"Hatch, we thought you'd been blown to bits by the British cannon. Are you hurt badly?"

James looked down at himself, and saw that his shirt was covered in blood. "Nay, I was not hit, to my knowledge. I was detained by a French surgeon to assist him in aiding the wounded and moving the dead."

He closed his eyes, suddenly weary and feeling near to tears. "Among those killed was Thomas, who helped us upon our arrival. He was a good man, sergeant, and I will miss him keenly."

"Aye, I spoke with him, as well. The chances of war are always difficult to bear when they strike down men we know."

James hesitated, and then decided to relay the surgeon's suggestion that he rest. "Doctor Perrault did not like how I looked, and told me to go and take some rest. Should I consult with our surgeon?"

The sergeant waved dismissively. "That won't be necessary. I can see as well as this Perrault that you are not yourself. Rest until supper, and let us see how tomorrow looks to you."

In his tent, James arranged himself on his bedroll, planning only to close his eyes for a minute. He jerked awake, though, to the sight of Thomas opening his eyes while he was being carried.

The Frenchman quipped in his distinctive accent, "Now you see that those British fellows aren't the only ones who can play tricks. I can walk on my own, but I like being carried like this well enough."

The dream had been vivid enough that it took James a few moments to shake it off and convince himself that it had not happened. No, Thomas would tell no more jokes, and would have no more opportunity to play tricks on anyone.

Patrick appeared at the entrance to the tent. "Sergeant told me to come fetch you for supper." He withdrew, and James raised himself from the bedroll, feeling as though the rest had done him no good at all. His legs felt leaden and were reluctant to respond to the commands of his mind, and his arms were like heavy ropes, hanging uselessly at his sides.

He gave himself a vicious shake, and forced his body to answer the demands he had of it. He was fortunate, he reminded himself. He still could walk and breathe and *feel*, and his skin was intact on a day when so many others had lost all of this and more.

He rolled his shoulders and slapped his cheeks, rousing

himself and exiting his tent into the waning sunlight. Patrick waited for him there, his expression inscrutable.

"Heard that that Frenchman Thomas got himself killed in the action today," he said. "I'd guess you are pretty torn up about that."

Of all the comments he expected from Patrick at the death of a mere Negro, this was near to the most improbable James could imagine. He answered, cautiously, "Yes, he was a friend and a good man."

Patrick snorted, shaking his head. "I suppose that I understand somewhat how you feel. After all, I can remember not feeling fully myself for days after my favorite dog died last year. This must be about the same for you."

James did not even consciously consider his response, so he was nearly as surprised as Patrick was when his fist connected with the other man's face. Patrick fell like a puppet with its strings cut, and James said nothing, barely even glancing back as he stepped over the man's prone form to go and eat.

Chapter 6

James expected some repercussions for striking out at Patrick the prior evening, and was on edge all day as he waited for the other shoe to drop. There had been no witnesses he was aware of — most everyone was clustered around the cook fires, eating supper — and he hadn't seen Patrick since he'd left him in the dirt.

He'd returned to working on the trench that had led to the prior day's disastrous British ambush, and was doing his best to not notice the places where the soil was stained dark with blood shed by its erstwhile defenders.

He was a little surprised to have been ordered to return to the position that had so clearly shown to be hazardous, but on reflection, he supposed that there was little likelihood that the British would attack in the same manner twice.

Besides, to abandon the hard-won work would be to waste the sacrifice that Thomas and the others buried yesterday had made. As he dug and piled soil, he concluded that completing the work that they had made possible was the best way that he could honor their memory.

Around mid-day, James saw Claude among the soldiers coming to relieve the guard that stood over them. He nodded gravely to the man, and Claude returned his nod, a somber expression on his face. There were no words needed between them, nor any practical across the language gap.

Claude turned a stony face to gaze toward the British earthworks, his eyes narrowing with obvious fury. The earth there bore scars from the action of the prior day, but James was relieved to see that Doctor Perrault's desire to recover the remaining casualties had been accomplished.

While he could accept that it might have been necessary, the thought of laboring here while fallen soldiers lay just over there was more than he thought he could bear. The mute stains on the walls and floor of the trench were sufficient reminder.

The late afternoon sun had reached high enough to finally warm James through when the squad that was to relieve his own arrived. Among their number was Patrick, his face swollen and battered-looking, but he barely even spared a glance for James.

What this could mean, James could not guess. He shrugged to himself, and set his shovel into the pile of soil he'd been adding to the berm and went back down through the trench toward the encampment.

As he passed Patrick, the man muttered something under his breath, and spat toward James' feet. For his part, James continued on as though he'd seen nothing.

He had answered Patrick in full already, in his estimation, and though he'd expected that he might face some official reprimand for it, none had materialized. He could only guess that for whatever inscrutable reason, Patrick had chosen not to bring the incident to the sergeant's attention.

He reached the cooking fire and held his hands out toward it to warm them. As the season advanced, the days were significantly less sweltering — which was a blessing when there was heavy work to be done — but the evenings had become downright chilly. He hoped that the siege here would be over before it got much colder.

He was focused on the flames in the cooking pit, and so didn't see the sergeant approach. "Hey there, Hatch. I hope you are feeling recovered from your ordeal of yesterday."

James looked up sharply, suddenly aware of the ache in his knuckles from where he'd struck Patrick, and wondering whether the sergeant was aware of that incident after all.

"I, uh, I'm feeling somewhat better today," he mumbled, adding, "I wish I had some French to be able to offer my sentiments to Thomas' companions, or that they had some English. I saw Claude today, standing guard in Thomas' place."

"'Tis a pity to have lost the services of someone capable of bridging that language barrier," the sergeant agreed. He looked at James' hands, still outstretched to catch the warmth of the fire.

"It appears that you were, in fact, injured in the course of yesterday's ambush," he noted.

James followed his glance and clasped his battered knuckles within the other palm. "Oh, I— I suppose I fell when the British cannon started firing," he lied, feeling a flush stealing over his face.

The sergeant did not notice . . . or if he did, chose not to comment. "Seems to be some of that going around. Another man in the company fell and broke his face pretty well — though it didn't manifest until later in the day."

He seemed lost in thought for a time, and James held his breath, waiting for the accusation he was certain would follow. Finally, the other man said, "War is a hazardous thing. Can cause all manner of strange and inexplicable injuries, some without leaving a mark."

James nodded. "I've heard of such things, though most of

the wounds I've witnessed have been plain enough to see."

The sergeant, pursing his mouth, said, "Aye, but those that cannot be seen can be just as destructive. A man can be changed forever by something that happens in a moment, or he can think himself unhurt, only to later discover that he has been mortally wounded."

James was no longer sure that he understood what the sergeant was getting at.

His uncertainty must have shown on his face, for after a glance at him, the man added, "I just want you to have a care that you have not been affected by what you've experienced, and that any hurts that this engagement may have inflicted on you do not wind up becoming mortal for lack of attention."

He turned to look James in the eye. "If there is aught that you need in order to preserve yourself, I would rather hear about it from you than be told about it at your graveside."

Thoroughly confused now, James said quickly, "I assure you, Sergeant, that I bear no wound that might lead you to have to bury me. I am as fit as a man can be under the circumstances." He ventured a quick grin, adding, "Although if the rations don't improve somewhat, there may be some risk, I suppose."

The sergeant acknowledged James' witticism with a small, tight smile. "I can make no promises as to rations. The Congress has yet to see fit to supply us decently, and I have no reason to suspect they might change that course."

He turned to leave, saying over his shoulder, "Mind your hand, Hatch, and if it shows any signs of getting worse, come and tell me before you risk further injury to it."

James nodded, wondering whether the sergeant had been

warning him against the dangers of fighting with his fellow soldiers through all of his comments, after all. He tossed his head to dispel the thought and joined the queue for some supper.

The next morning, stamping about in the chill before breakfast was served out, trying to warm up his feet in the worn, thin excuses for shoes that he'd been issued, James was surprised to hear the lieutenant call his name.

"Private Hatch, a word, if you can be spared."

James spun to face the officer, saluted and answered, "Of course, sir." It was bad enough that the sergeant had taken an interest in him, but now the officers of the company knew him by name? That could portend nothing good. Perhaps his fisticuffs with Patrick had finally come to official attention.

The lieutenant led him away to a quiet spot from the breakfast crowd, and said, "In light of their losses, our French allies have asked for a detail of men to assist with guard patrols over the trench construction. Your sergeant recommended that I have you take this duty. I presume you can make yourself available?"

"Aye, sir." James relaxed just the tiniest bit as he realized that he was not in trouble, but was, in fact, being offered a relief from the hard labor of digging and earthmoving. Pacing about the earthworks had to be easier than digging through sod and packing down the berm.

Then he remembered how many of the guards had died just two days before, and swallowed hard. Easier duty, perhaps, but riskier. The lieutenant did not notice this evidence of nerves on James' part, though, and nodded his approval.

"Good. We will find someone in their ranks who can speak English enough to acquaint you with the commands you must be alert to. Your sergeant said that you do not speak any French. Is that right?"

James replied, "Right, sir, I have no French, but I will endeavor to learn what I need to be able to take part in the drill."

The lieutenant's expression grew grim. "It's no drill, Hatch, as you know from the late events at the trench. That does remind me, though, that I'll have to remember to have them show you what differences there may be in the firing sequence, should it come to that."

James swallowed again, and this time the lieutenant spotted his bobbing Adam's apple.

He chuckled. "Don't worry, Private. If there should be fighting while you are amidst the French line, it is likely to be just as chaotic and confused as anything you would see on the American line. Just keep your musket supplied, and the balls headed toward the enemy, and you'll be fine."

"Aye, sir, that I can do."

"I trust that you can, Hatch." The officer clapped him on the shoulder. "There are a couple of other men I need to speak with who will be with you in this duty, and then I'll accompany you over to the French officer who asked for you. Go and eat your breakfast — you'll continue to mess with your company, and sleep here when your watch is done, naturally."

The officer departed at a brisk walk, and James wondered at the energy he had for this hour of the day.

After eating his breakfast of thin porridge — the cook swore it had some salt pork in it today — James gathered up his musket and the rest of his kit. He opened the top of his cartridge bag and felt the paper of each cartridge, confirming that they remained dry and ready, before he closed and secured it again.

He'd seen that the guard patrols kept their bayonets fixed, but decided that he would wait until he was told to do that. Doctrine — American doctrine, at least — advised that they should not be routinely left so, lest someone on your own side should unintentionally find the point in a scramble.

Slinging and adjusting his musket and bags, James looked about for the lieutenant and found him with a knot of other men at the edge of the American encampment.

The officer looked him over with approval, and addressed those gathered. "All right, that's all of you. Let's go over and find Captain Dozois. He'll be in charge of you lot, and will see to anything you might need."

He pronounced the French officer's name "*Doze-wah*," and James thought privately that it was as odd-sounding a name as he had yet encountered in getting to know their allies.

Looking over the group as they proceeded through the French tents, James was struck anew by the contrast between the crisp, well-tailored uniforms of the French units they passed by and the worn, comparatively untidy, and varied outfits of the Americans.

The observation might have made him feel ashamed, but instead, he found that he rather liked the individuality of the American appearance. They each wore cocked hats of heavy black felt, and while none had succumbed to the fashion of tucking feathers into them or any such macaroni nonsense, but even in this simple matter of standard uniform, there were individual touches.

James' own hat was so old that it was noticeably paler than most — at some point, he ought to engage the services of a milliner to re-black it — while another man in their group had evidently sprung for a brand-new hat . . . and recently, too. Its folds were more well-defined and its fabric smoother than those on the heads of the men around him.

More important, though, was what the American soldiers had in common. Their muskets were in good order, and their general comportment reflected a sense of pride and duty. James could see several other men in the detail looking around as they passed through the French encampment, and wondered if they were noticing the same things he was.

The group reached a French officer whose uniform was even more crisply turned out than the rest of the allies, and the American lieutenant offered him a relaxed salute.

"Lieutenant Miller, sir, with the requested troops for guard duty."

The French officer returned the salute with what seemed to James like exaggerated care, and spoke with a thick Gallic accent. "I thank you for your willingness to supply men for this crucial duty." The smile that he offered did not reach even the corners of his mouth, never mind his eyes. "I will see to it that they are well employed and returned to your encampment at the end of their shift."

The lieutenant saluted once more in answer and left without saying anything further.

Their temporary commander looked them over and said something in French that James did not understand. He looked around at the men expectantly, and then said, "I suppose it was too much to hope that one of you might speak any French. Ah, well." He shrugged and motioned for the men to follow him.

Straggling along behind him, looking more like an assortment of lost sheep than a squad of soldiers, the Americans shared glances that reflected the misgivings James was feeling. The lieutenant had said that they would be taught the French they needed, yet this officer made them feel inadequate for not already having it.

The French captain called out to a small man whose face was marked with a vicious scar, stretching from the hairline above one eye, across his nose, and down to the far side of his chin. While his scar gave his visage a fierce appearance, the man had gentle eyes, and for some reason, James liked him on sight.

The captain held a brief conversation with the scarred Frenchman, and when they were through, he turned back to the American troops. "Corporal Prevard will teach you all that you need to know. Thank you for your assistance."

Prevard stepped forward and said briskly, and with a light accent that James couldn't place, "Welcome. I am not familiar with the drill on which your regiments may have trained, so I will start from the assumption that you know nothing. This is not meant as an insult, but only so that we are all starting from the same point."

He unslung the musket from his back, and James was surprised to see the corporal's entire carriage change. Where he had been casual and relaxed in his tone and movements before, now he was all business. The gentleness that James had seen in his eyes was gone, and he had no trouble at all imagining Corporal Prevard as a killer of men.

"Your muskets are very similar to ours, so I will not waste time teaching you the names of the parts, and what they all do. I will trust that you know that much, at least."

He flashed a smile, and then his expression regained its serious nature. "I will show you the commands and steps we use in prepare, load, fire, and clear our guns. Unsling your guns and follow along, but do not use a cartridge."

He smiled again, for the briefest of moments, but there was a hard edge to it now. "There is no need to alarm your compatriots, lest they open fire on us again." James cringed. Clearly, all was not forgiven.

By the time the sun had risen to the highest point it would manage this late in the year, the squad was responding well enough to the commands Prevard barked at them in French that he announced himself satisfied that they could assume their duties.

He marched them over to the end of the entrenchment where men labored to bring it ever nearer to the British positions, and spoke to the leader of the guards on duty there. He turned back to introduce the soldier to the American squad, but James knew Claude as soon as he saw his friend's face.

Chapter 7

"Corporal Legrand and I will be your *bas-officiers* while you are on guard duty," Prevard said. "However, Legrand will be the man calling out commands, should the need arise."

He made a comment to Claude, who laughed and shook his head before answering. "Corporal Legrand has as little English as you all have French, unfortunately, but he tells me that he has worked with some of you before."

Claude added something and pointed to James. Prevard's eyebrows shot up, and he conversed in rapid-fire French with Claude for a moment longer before addressing James.

"Legrand tells me that you were present when Private Lambert was killed."

James nodded, reluctantly. "I was, I am sad to say."

Prevard gave James an inscrutable look, and then said, "Doctor Perrault told me about the events of that day. He related a story that I found striking, based on the way that some of our soldiers have been treated."

James said nothing, his head lowered in emotion as he recalled the horrible moment when Thomas breathed his last.

Prevard continued after a pause. "It was a very Christian thing you did, attending to Lambert in his last breaths, and taking care of him after he was gone. We would all do well to so minister to any person who falls, whether they are like us or not."

James looked up then, and fixed Prevard with a flinty gaze. "I don't see how Private Lambert was any different from you or me. He was a good man, who found happiness wherever he could, and who gave his life in the service of my country. Ministering to him, as you say, was the very least I could do, and I would do likewise for any man under the same circumstances."

Prevard didn't say anything immediately, but met James' eyes before nodding slowly in agreement. He said, "I take your point, Private. In any case, Corporal Legrand asked me to tell you that he is grateful to you for taking care of his friend and comrade."

James looked at Claude and dipped his chin in acknowledgment of the soldier's grief. "Please convey to Corporal Legrand my sorrow that I could not save Private Lambert. These men are some of the finest I have yet come to know in either the American or the French armies."

Prevard translated for James, and Claude's expression reflected the loss that James understood he must be feeling.

Filling the silence that followed, Prevard said, briskly, "There is work to be done now. The time for remembering fallen friends is after we have completed their duties in their stead."

He straightened his own slumped shoulders and continued, "Each of you will pair yourself with a French soldier for the last hour of our patrol, and when they have pointed out the particular hazards of their locations, you will relieve them, and we will ensure that the rest of the day's work is not interrupted by our rude and restive neighbors invested within the town. Find your posts, men."

Claude pointed to James and motioned for him to stay with the corporals as the rest of the men dispersed along the length of the entrenchment. James joined him and Prevard, and as they walked the section of the trench for which Claude was evidently responsible, the two French soldiers conversed in low tones.

James thought he saw Claude stop on at least one occasion to wipe away a tear, but neither he nor Prevard opted to explain what they were discussing.

The afternoon passed without any appearances from the British, and at the end of their patrol, Prevard approached James.

He said, "If your company can spare you this evening, Legrand would like for you to join us for a drink, perhaps a bite to eat. Our provisions are no longer very good, but he tells me that his friend thought that they were perhaps still a bit better than what you are eating?"

James grinned sardonically. "Water from the swamp would probably be better than what we are eating these days. I would be most pleased to join you, and need only secure the permission of my sergeant to do so."

Prevard laughed, and when he translated for Claude, the other man also erupted in a roar of amusement.

"Very well," Prevard said. "It cannot be that hard to convince your superiors to leave some more swamp water for your fellows, no?"

When James consulted his sergeant, the man grunted, "Suit yourself. But mind that you don't forget which army you fight for in the end. Those Frenchmen are our allies today, but make no mistake — it is a matter of circumstances only."

Soberly, James said, "I have not forgotten, sir. They are but fellow soldiers in our shared fight."

In the French encampment, Prevard welcomed James to sit

around the cooking fire. He pressed a bottle into his hand, and urged, "Drink one for the memory of your friend, and one for your own sake, too."

James accepted the offering and sniffed of it. "Is this rum?"

"Oh, yes, from Saint-Domingue itself. A better rum you'll not taste, either."

James took a cautious sip, and his mouth burned as though it had been set on fire. He gasped and choked, desperately handing the bottle back to Prevard, who was doubled over in laughter.

The other man gathered himself sufficiently to accept the rum, and then resumed laughing when James fell into a fresh fit of coughing.

When Prevard could speak again, he wheezed, "Likely you'll not taste a stronger rum, either. I hear that what we sell for export is given plenty of water before any of it reaches the markets beyond Cap-Français."

He fortified himself with another swig from the bottle, smacking his lips in a show of how tasty it was. "I had never had any this good before I came to know our regiments from Saint-Domingue, but I cannot guess how I will go back to what I drank at home."

James had recovered enough to be able to speak again, and asked, "Where is home, then, if not on Saint-Domingue?"

"Oh, I grew up in a small town in mother France."

"But you speak such perfect English that I can sometimes scarcely remember you are French."

"Ah, well, there is a story there, let me assure you . . . though not one that I can freely share. What I can tell you is that I spent a fair amount of time in, let us say, close examination of the British shipyards. You see, King Louis thought it prudent to have a clear idea of what sort of projects our friends had underway."

He touched the scar on his face, and his voice lowered. "Not everyone I met felt it was so good an idea for people beyond their own shores to be well acquainted with the innovations they were engaged in."

He belched quietly, and added, "Such damnable innovations, too. Some were mere entertainments, but others . . . Our friends in the Navy were happy enough to sink, burn or take, when the opportunity presented itself."

He raised the bottle up above head level and spoke more loudly now. "But we are not here to discuss ancient intelligences or gossip about naval design. We are here to remember our valiant lost men, brought to ruin by those selfsame British tricksters."

Claude approached from behind Prevard then, and plucked the bottle out of his hand with a happy smile. He made a comment that even James could tell was sarcastic by the tone with which he spoke.

But Prevard gathered himself to clumsily rush at his compatriot, forcing Claude to cut short his pull at the bottle and quickly hand it off to James. Claude then pivoted out of Prevard's path at the last possible moment, so that Prevard stumbled and tripped, skidding to the ground with an impact that made James wince.

Prevard only rolled over, laughing uproariously, and Claude waved his hands, taunting the other man to make another run at him.

Instead, Prevard stood up and shook his head, still laughing. He said something to Claude and offered his hand in apparent conciliation — but when Claude accepted it with a merry grin on his face, Prevard pulled him abruptly forward and put a foot into his way, tripping Claude and sending him sprawling in the dirt.

Claude rolled with more grace than had Prevard, and let the momentum of his fall carry him to spring up onto his feet once more, laughing wildly himself. Prevard bowed graciously to him, pointedly keeping his hands tucked behind himself, and Claude returned the honor.

Watching their antics, James risked another sip of rum, and found it just as potent the second time. It did not set off a second round of choking, though, as he was braced for it this time.

Prevard spotted him drinking from the bottle and held out his hand for its return, his expression suddenly serious. With the rum gripped tightly in his hand, he raised one finger of the other hand. "We drink once for memory." He illustrated by way of example and then raised a second finger. "Twice for revenge. Again, he demonstrated, a deep scowl in his eyes as his throat worked to swallow the harsh liquor.

Raising a third finger, he said, slowly, "And a third time for . . . oh, what is the word? *Fraternité* . . . ah, yes — brotherhood!"

He tipped the bottle up over his head and drank another healthy gulp, then handed it to Claude, who repeated the gestures, but who spoke only in French. "*Memoire . . . et revenge . . . et fraternité.*"

Claude offered the bottle to James again, and Prevard held up a hand. "Before you drink again, let me explain that this is the rum of the oath. To give it that power, it is mixed with a bit of gunpowder, and to swear by it binds you to a sacred bond. Will you drink of it of your own free will?"

James looked at him steadily and raised a finger. "Memory." A second finger. "Revenge." The third finger rose, and he caught both Claude and Prevard's eyes before he said, firmly, "Brotherhood," and finished the bottle.

James remembered very little about the rest of the night, save that he was insistent that he must be returned to the American encampment after supper.

Based on the evidence beside his bedroll when he awoke in the morning, it would have been better had he skipped supper entirely. Whatever it had been was wasted on him, and if it were as good as Prevard had intimated, he had no memory of savoring the taste.

He groaned as his sergeant kicked his foot. "Up, Hatch. You're a disgrace, and I won't soon let you spend time with those French soldiers after duty hours again, but your squad cannot spare you from your guard detail."

James looked up at the sergeant through squinted eyes, his head pounding a tattoo that felt as though he were standing right beside one of the great water drums that the Shawnee used for their dances.

"You've already missed your breakfast, not that you look as though you would be able to keep that down, and your squad will be going over to the entrenchments in a few minutes, so get yourself up and presentable. Get moving, private."

The sergeant did not wait around to see whether James actually did get up, but turned on his heel, wrinkling his nose as he did.

On his way out of the tent, he tossed over his shoulder, "Clean up your mess before you go, too."

As James worked to remove the remnants of his supper from the tent floor, he recalled snatches of the prior evening's conversations. At one point, he had demanded of Claude, through Prevard, what he knew of Henri's fate. Claude had frowned and related that Henri was performing menial labor, as he'd had some kind of confrontation with the commander of their regiment.

Claude seemed to feel that Henri's punishment was in retribution for Henri having pointed out a thing that was self-evident — that the men of the *Chasseurs-Volontaires* were deserving of the same treatment in all matters as any of the other troops. Count d'Estaing himself had published detailed orders to that effect, but it seemed to have little practical application, so far as his subordinate officers were concerned.

James remembered feeling relief that Henri had been spared at the British walls, but not fully understanding what the conflict was that Henri had gotten involved in.

He had a confused memory, too, that at another point, he'd insisted that his companions drink a toast to the nobility of the American officers. They had thought he was jesting, and had burst into giggles.

Only true brotherhood restrained James' response at that show of disrespect, but it had been no more than a passing irritation.

There was more, as well, but it was lost in a swirl of things that James could not be sure had actually happened, and many that he was quite certain had not. It seemed vanishingly unlikely, for example, that nobody would have stopped them from jumping up to the top of the French earthworks to expose their backsides to the British by the light of the moon.

James dismissed this clearly illusory recollection, finished the foul work at hand, and made his way as quickly as he could over to the French encampment, to report for his shift on guard duty.

Prevard and Claude looked as though they shared the agony that James was feeling to some degree, but both were at least clean and shaved . . . which was a bit more than James could claim for himself. He was aware of how he must smell, though, given that both of the French corporals whiffed of an ale-house.

Prevard greeted him with a wry smile. "Brotherhood comes at a price sometimes, eh?" Claude shook his head ruefully, and the trio fell into step together toward their designated patrol.

Happily, the day was uneventful, and none of the three of them had much to say until that afternoon, when Prevard spoke up, motioning at the ongoing digging and berm-building. "What do you suppose the plan will be?"

James looked at the French soldier sharply. "Why, I've no idea. Our generals are not in the habit of sharing their plans with mere private soldiers such as myself. I suppose they will inform us of what we are to do next when the time comes."

Prevard nodded thoughtfully. "I have heard rumors that our general is eager to launch an assault on the British positions, I know that our supplies are growing thin — the meals have only gotten worse in the past several days — and it does not seem that the British lack for resolve to outlast us."

"If anything, their attack on us demonstrates that they are confident enough to risk wasting men and supplies in the effort," James reasoned, glad for a distraction from the lingering ache in his head. At least now, the thought of supper did not make him want to retch.

"A good observation," Prevard noted. "Our generals have us continuing to push the trenches ever closer to the British lines, despite that assault, which has me wondering how long they intend to try to wait out the enemy."

"I am not eager to try those defenses." James motioned at the abattis, and the redoubts visible beyond them. "They've had time to prepare quite thoroughly, it seems."

Prevard bristled. "There is no truth to the rumor that Admiral d'Estaing made a mistake by letting the British commander have a twenty-hour hour truce after demanding his surrender. It was completely unforeseeable that the would have been able to reinforce so quickly, or marshal the labor available to him to complete these fortifications."

James held up his hands in surrender. "I meant no insult to your Admiral d'Estaing. Indeed, I had not previously heard of these events, only that your troops landed last week, not waiting for our arrival to establish the siege."

He did not add that he'd overheard some officers angrily discussing dark suspicions that the French commander was planning to simply seize this territory for France, rather than act in actual alliance with the Americans.

Prevard took a deep breath, seeming to master his earlier irritation, and he shrugged lightly. "The Admiral saw an opportunity and seized it." He grinned merrily, adding, "It is not our fault that our British friends failed to play their part in the plan."

Then he laughed, the scar on his face contorting around his grin, and Claude looked at him quizzically.

The two French soldiers conversed briefly as Prevard explained what he'd been talking with James about.

He turned back to James and said, "Legrand thinks we're going to wind up trying to attack. We have been unable to move our heavy guns from the ships, lacking the horses and heavy carriages required to do so, but he spoke to a friend in the artillery company."

He pursed his lips briefly in contemplation, and added, "That fellow told him that they have now been able to find what they needed and will be moving their guns into position soon. In fact, the carriages are being built by some of our local sympathizers, just as quickly as they can knock them together."

James answered slowly, "While I would rather simply keep them hemmed in long enough to starve the British out, I will confess that it would do my heart good to return some of the weight of metal they threw against your men."

Prevard grinned. "Yes, some well-aimed cannon balls would be most satisfying, would they not? Pound for pound, with substantial increase for the price in blood theirs exacted."

He slapped his hands against his hips by way of emphasis and added, "But these are not our decisions to make, are they? We will need to wait and see what the generals think is prudent, which will likely depend upon how thin their own rations grow, as much as anything else."

Chapter 8

The routine of rising, messing for breakfast with the troops from his own company, and then marching over to join Prevard's detail in guard duty had become almost dull. It varied only in whether the day would offer a downpour to make them miserable as they marched to and fro along the lines, or the air would be so heavy and humid that their own sweat would drench their clothes by the end of the watch.

However, on this morning, an excited buzz at the cooking fire promised some relief from that repetitive cycle, and James joined the queue for food with his ears perked up for the latest gossip.

A man he did not know was speaking to one of his squad mates, his voice carrying clearly across the crowd.

"We detected a British detachment — numbering more than two hundred men — trying to sneak in, with the clear object of reinforcing the garrison within the town. They unloaded from five ships near to where we were placed. I suppose they determined that the French fleet here would not permit them to come into the town itself by water."

He held up his hands to signal for patience in response to the growls of resolve at the revelation that the enemy had been so bold as to try to bring yet more men into the town. "Don't you worry, there was no chance at all they were going to be able to make it here by land, either, with Colonel White in between them and their destination. Wait until you hear how we stopped them."

Warming to his subject, he continued, "Now, bear in mind that it was just the colonel, a couple of his officers, the three of us privates, and our sergeant, with hundreds of those lobsterbacks in front of us in the woods. The colonel knew that the only way we could stop them would be to trick them."

Someone scoffed, and a voice called out from the soldiers surrounding the storyteller. "Why didn't he just send someone back here to get a larger detachment from our regiment?"

The man shook his head dismissively. "There was no time, I tell you. Instead, the colonel had us all spread out around the British position, and lay fires, to make it appear as though they had stumbled into the middle of the encampment of the whole American army."

He illustrated their placement around the British force with motions of his hands. "Then, the colonel had and move about the fires, calling orders out to the supposed army camped all about us, commanding them to make ready to take the British who had dared to land amongst us."

He grinned now, clearly relishing the chuckles that arose around him. "Then the colonel marched out of the darkness into their midst, bold as brass, and demanded to speak to their commanding officer, so as to negotiate the terms of their surrender."

"And they fell for it?"

"As hard as if they had been thrown from an unbroken stallion." He chortled and added, "Let me tell you, though, they were a little surprised when it was just the seven of us who came out of the woods to escort them back to confinement."

One man interjected, "I'll bet they were!"

The soldier's voice was even more filled with mirth as he added, "That's not all, either. Colonel White even convinced them that it was hopeless for their ships to attempt escape, and so we took all five of those, as well, with their crews and guns and all. He got their leader to sign his articles of capitulation before the sun could rise and reveal our deception."

He grinned joyfully, and said, "When we marched them through the 'camps' and they saw that there was nothing to them but a few smoldering fires, let me tell you, they were more than a little dismayed, and it was some kind of doings to persuade them that they must abide by the terms of their surrender, despite outnumbering us by better than twenty men to our every one."

Shaking his head in disbelief, James kept his opinions to himself, but he was clearly not alone in doubting that the man's story was not a wild exaggeration. Privately, he thought it likely that the captured British force had been no more than a few dozen men, and that the ruse Colonel White had employed had barely been necessary to overcome them.

Others were not so reticent to share their doubts, so their own lieutenant eventually emerged from his tent, his expression triumphant, and shouted down the questioners. "Colonel White has accomplished an act of daring and bravery scarcely equaled in all this army. Why, I should not be surprised if he is still being toasted and recounted one hundred years hence. Three cheers for Colonel White!"

The company raised three ragged cheers at the lieutenant's urging, and the officer returned to his tent, satisfied. The soldier who'd told the story looked smugly pleased with himself, while those who'd been challenging him seemed to remember as a body that they were there to break their fasts, and turned to speak amongst themselves.

For his own part, James still harbored some skepticism as to the magnitude of the victory, but was glad to be able to bring word of it over to his French detail mates.

When he arrived to begin his shift on guard duty, Claude and Prevard both seemed in high spirits already. Without preamble, Prevard said, "So, I heard news that one of your patrols had a very good night, and that the British had their pride dented a bit."

"Aye, that they did," James answered, feeling a little deflated that the news had reached his friends before he could deliver it himself. However, that feeling passed quickly when Prevard added, "Tell me what you have heard, and I will share it with Corporal Legrand. I am sure you have more details than we here have heard."

James related the American private's report about the encounter between his squad and the British in the night, and Prevard provided a running translation for Claude's sake.

When James was finished with the story, Prevard nodded somberly. "Our British friends will be in a foul mood today, presuming that the news has reached their ears. The taking of two of their ships and three merchants besides will not have gone unnoticed, I am certain."

James agreed, "We shall need to be on our guard today, lest they try to strike a blow in vengeance for this embarrassment. Their patience has been keenly tried already, and this is the sort of thing that can drive a man to the breaking point."

"You make a sound observation," Prevard nodded. "It may only be a matter of time before their patience can bear no more provocation."

He grinned. "So, naturally, we will soon be offering them further provocations, some eight and twelve pounds at a time, in the form of cannon balls to prevent them from venturing out from behind their earthworks, or even sleeping, for that matter."

"How do the preparations go for the great guns?"

"The general himself has been laboring alongside the men, to ensure that we all understand how important the emplacements of the cannon are to his plans."

Prevard winked at James and added, "The provisions at his table must have become poor indeed for him to have decided that it is now urgent to force the question."

James chuckled, but he could not completely suppress his own disquiet at the prospect of open battle against the enemy.

Numbers, at least, were on their side, but that was no assurance of carrying the day. The cannon emplacements of the British were, to his unpracticed eye, well-sited to be difficult to strike, and he had already witnessed their effectiveness.

There was one spot along the British earthworks that looked as though the lay of the land was more favorable to the besiegers than to the defenders, but James had no doubt that their foes were just as keenly aware of the exposure, and that they had made more robust preparations there as a result.

Any other avenue of attack was likely to be at least as well defended as the site where the French had stumbled into an ambush, and James did not like at all the thought of trying their luck against those defenses another time.

He said nothing of this to Prevard, though, offering only, "I wonder how thin the provisions have grown for our enemies, if our own have reached such desperate straits?"

Prevard shrugged, his brows lifted in emphasis. "It is impossible for us to know, but I imagine they must be even more eager than we are to see this siege come to its conclusion."

"How long do you suppose it might be, then?"

Prevard shrugged again. "We may be able to exercise the big guns in another day or two, and certainly we will be able to start bombarding the town within the week. What the results of that might be is very difficult to guess, as it will depend on the luck and skill of our gunners, and the resolve of the defenders within. I have heard of sieges broken when a singly lucky ball struck down a senior officer, and I have heard of sieges that went on for days on end without a clear outcome."

He looked around at the French encampment. "I believe that we are, despite the complaints at the officers' tables, relatively well supplied to be able to hold the British within the walls of this town for quite some time. And even that may be extended, if your countrymen can be depended upon to offer us fresh provisions, while denying the enemy all possible resupply."

James smiled grimly. "At least your ships prevent any relief to the British by water. And our presence here should bar any possibility of supplies entering by land — even if we must resort to subterfuge to accomplish that goal, as Colonel White did."

Claude asked something in French, and Prevard explained to him what they were discussing. He scowled and made a short comment to Prevard, who relayed his sentiment.

"Corporal Legrand believes that our general is more desirous of a quick victory, so that he can retire to his estates in France without dishonor, and that he does not care how many men he sacrifices to achieve his own benefit."

Prevard shook his head, grimacing. "Of course, it is ever so with generals. The fates of the individual soldiers under their commands are of little interest to them in their schemes and calculations, and they are most interested in their own advancement and reputation. I have little doubt that Legrand is likely right about this."

He squared his shoulders. "But! Enough gossip and belly-aching. I know it is the favorite activity of every soldier from Caesar's day to this, but we have an entrenchment to guard."

Chapter 9

James had never been near a full-throated cannonade before, and the pounding of the great guns was something both magnificent and awful to behold. The crashing and booming had begun in the middle of the night, and continued through the morning, with occasional pauses only to let the guns cool.

To his eye, as the light rose enough to let him see, it did appear that the French gun crews were less organized and methodical about their work than the average line of muskets, but that hardly seemed to matter when the balls went smashing through the town.

He supposed that more disciplined aiming and firing might have had more focused effects on the British emplacements, and could have rained less destruction down upon the town that they were supposedly trying to liberate from enemy occupation . . . but he admitted to himself that he knew little about how accurate a gun that size might be able to be.

After all, a musket ball could only be aimed in the general direction of an enemy line, not at a specific man on the line, so it might well be that the much larger guns had proportionally much larger margins of error.

However, as he walked across the encampment to find a better vantage point to see around the clouds of dense gun-smoke that had gathered around the cannon emplacements, he came upon a knot of American artillery men. Their disparaging comments about the quality of the French gunnery made his heart sink.

"For the love of all that's holy, if that's how they intend to treat this unfortunate town, there won't be anything left for the British to relinquish by the time they're done," one man was saying as James approached.

Another shook his head sadly. "When we must attack on foot, the enemy's cannon will be free to wreak havoc upon our lines, so little damage is being done to them by this gunnery."

A third man was even blunter in his assessment. "Why, a child could make better aim than those French gunners. The effect of their fire makes it appear that they are all drunk."

James said nothing, but he suspected this last comment might be close to the truth. While he had not been in the French encampment since the disastrous evening of the rum oath, he knew from that experience that there seemed to be little objection to drinking when off duty, even if it might affect one's on-duty performance later.

The first artillery man exclaimed as a column of smoke started to rise from within the town. "Now they've gone and set a fire in town. I suppose if this were a French town, their generals might exercise a bit more discipline, but since's it's just an American town, why not blast it full of holes, and reduce the entire thing to ash, while they're at it?" He spat disdainfully.

James ventured to speak up then. "Do you think that they are fully in control of how much damage their shots inflict upon the innocents trapped in town with the enemy? I do not know a great deal about cannon, but should they be any more reliable than a musket?"

The soldier turned to him and scoffed, "The great guns can

be aimed with far more consistency than a musket. After all, they are placed on a steady carriage, and while they must be elevated and pointed with care for the wind and distance, once that is done, one ball will land practically atop the prior, so long as the position of the gun is restored accurately between shots."

He motioned with his chin at the musket slung over his own shoulder. "A man moves about too much to achieve the same result, never mind that the tiniest variation in how much powder is loaded will change the trajectory of a musket ball quite a lot. When we load powder into a cannon, a difference of a few grains won't make a tremendous change in the strength of the charge."

He motioned with a sardonic expression toward the French cannon battery, which just then fired again, a gout of flame erupting from the muzzle of one gun after another in sequence. Speaking quickly, before the sound of the barrage could overcome his words, he said, "These fellows seem to be off by more than a few mere grains of powder from one shot to the next."

After the thunder of the cannonade had rolled over them, the group watched to see whether they could spot where the balls had struck. Their position did not afford them a view into the town — which was on higher ground than its surroundings — but they looked out of force of habit, and in the hopes that the French gun crews might have improved their aim to strike at the British redoubts.

To a man, the artillerymen groaned as the enemy positions stood unmarked by the balls, which crashed into the town beyond. The sounds of that destruction were masked, though, by another French battery firing its own round of shot. The men watched without comment for several more rounds before James inclined his head respectfully to the American artillery troops and moved on.

Since the cannon barrage had started, the guard patrols around the entrenchments had been dropped, and he'd had no opportunity to visit his friends in the French camp. However, having finished the duty his sergeant had assigned him for the day — ominously, preparing and packing cartridges for muskets, in preparation for what could only be an assault in force on the British positions — James found himself for the first time in a couple of days with a few free minutes at his disposal.

He made his way over to the French encampment, despite challenges from guards who were significantly more alert than they had been prior to the beginning of actual offensive operations, and wove through the now-familiar rows of French tents. He sought out Corporal Prevard, and found him methodically disassembling and cleaning his musket.

The French soldier raised a hand in greeting, but said nothing as he continued the routine, but exacting job. James returned Prevard's wave and sat down to wait for his friend to be ready to speak with him.

As he waited, Claude appeared and offered James a friendly smile. Then, he sat down beside Prevard and began stripping his own musket.

In combination with his assignment at preparing cartridges, the sight of the two French soldiers carefully preparing their weapons for action should have left James feeling unsettled at the prospect that the arms might soon be needed, but he found that it gave him comfort, instead.

His own musket had long since been cleaned, serviced, and prepared. Of course, he had put few enough rounds through the barrel since it was issued to him that the weapon had not really had a chance to develop much in the way of a distinct character.

He knew some men who had served with the same weapon for years, and described how this one needed a little extra coaxing to clear its borehole after a shot, or that one needed a light hand with the ramrod, but his gun had never been anything but reliable and predictable.

Prevard turned the screws to tighten down the last of the fittings for his gun's barrel, gave everything one last inspection, and then slung it over his shoulder, before standing and reaching out to take James' hand in greeting.

"They say that we may try the enemy as soon as tomorrow, depending upon what results our artillery gets."

The Frenchman shook his head, grimacing so deeply that the scar across his face nearly disappeared into the lines around his mouth. "If the crews at the guns had spent less time last night drinking to their victory, and more time preparing for it, I might have more faith that we would be undertaking that assault so soon as some have tried to convince us it would be happening."

James admitted, "I had wondered at the performance of the gun crews. Even from our lines, it appeared that they were doing poorly at controlling where their shots fell."

Prevard scowled. "Yes, and it is quite frustrating to those of us who are depending on their gunnery to reduce the enemy's defenses, to see them instead doing great violence to the town that has the bad fortune of being within their siege lines. Rather than facing smashed and demoralized emplacements, we may be going up against the full fury of Britain's best-trained troops. At the same time, those within the town who might have been predisposed toward the British have now been given reason to oppose us by all possible means."

"Is there no way to prevail upon them to cease firing until they have recovered their capabilities?"

Prevard frowned, looking away at to where Claude was just slipping the trigger mechanism out of its position within the stock of his musket. "No, their commander has insisted that imperfect fire is better than none at all, now that we have commenced the attack. I suppose the theory is that a cessation of the bombardment would give the British forces time to regain their shattered wits, and perhaps even mount a counterattack. As it is, the idea goes, they are so well occupied with avoiding each incoming round that they have no time to fire their own cannonades at us."

He grinned sarcastically, and added, "It is nonsense, of course. The British won't waste shots now on anything short of a mass attack of troops. With the help of your forces, as we saw with Colonel White's *coup de main* a few days ago, we have shown that they must not rely on being able to receive either supplies or any more men within our cordon."

He shrugged, adding a self-deprecating gesture. "Of course, what do I know, a lowly corporal? All of the really important assessments and decisions are being made by the generals and their staffs, based upon what they can learn, and we are to but carry out their commands."

He gestured toward where Claude was loosening the screws that held in the brackets around his musket's barrel. "And so, we prepare for anything that might happen, and hope that none of it does."

Another ripple of thundering cannon fire rolled over the

landscape, and James returned Prevard's grimace. "Perhaps the effects achieved by the gun crews will improve as the day goes on, or by the break of morning tomorrow, to the point that we will not even need to undertake an assault of our own."

Prevard grinned, without humor. "Perhaps, but perhaps also King George will grow wings and fly out of the palace and into the sun, never again to torment us on this Earth."

He shook his head. "No, my friend, we must be resigned to the fact that the hour approaches when we will need to place ourselves in the path of the enemy's bullets, and directly contest for this unfortunate town."

James sighed, and watched Claude sight down the detached barrel of his musket, before running a cleaning wad through it one last time.

"I know you are right, and yet I cannot help but wish there were some way we could avoid that dire eventuality. No matter how well we outnumber the enemy, I cannot escape the memory of those who fell in that skirmish. These British soldiers are more determined and more clever than I think some of our officers give them credit for."

Prevard closed his eyes in remembered pain, and said, quietly, "It would be even better if we did not help them to kill our soldiers."

James shot him a quizzical look. "How's that?"

"It has been little remarked upon outside of a few who were there to witness it, but I have heard from more than one person that the reason we were fooled into that cannon ambush at the entrenchments was that the colonel who led us out to pursue the British excursion was emboldened not only by the enemy's feigned vulnerability, but also by an excess of rum."

He made a disgusted noise, and waved in the direction of the gun batteries as they discharged yet another barrage. "The same incapacitation that afflicts our gun crews today led to the destruction of many dozens of good men."

The Frenchman grimaced, but his eyes held a glint of dark humor. "If the British want to defeat us, they would do better to send us a wagon loaded full of rum than to answer any of these cannonades with shot."

James' laughter carried an edge of regret in it. "I can testify to the effectiveness that strategy would have, from personal experience. I should not have been capable of effectively handling anything more complex than a knife the morning after our rum oath — and I would have been nearly as dangerous to myself as to the enemy."

Prevard offered him a half-smile, but it faded quickly. "In any event, we may be on the brink of being able to fulfill that oath to avenge Thomas' death, taking blood for blood from the British butchers who killed him."

Claude looked up at the mention of Thomas' name. "*Memoire, et revenge, et fraternité,*" he intoned, catching James' glance with a gaze that suddenly burned with intensity. James acknowledged him with a bare nod of his head, and Claude looked back down at his weapon, which he was now reassembling methodically.

"Soon," James said. "I am eager in particular for the vengeance portion."

Another cannonade sounded, this time followed by a few shouts of encouragement to the gun crew.

James looked out toward the town and spotted a second column of smoke rising, seeming closer to the British line.

"Perhaps very soon," he added, and Prevard nodded in agreement.

Chapter 10

It was nearly impossible to sleep with the French guns roaring their challenge toward the British lines throughout the night. Of course, James reflected, it had to be harder to sleep at the other end of the cannon's aim than behind the French line — and that was without a doubt, part of the strategy.

Still, the sound penetrated every tent in the encampment, and James could tell by the dark circles under many eyes, and more short-tempered comments than usual in the queue at the breakfast mess that he was not the only one who had gotten little sleep for all the din. He spotted the artillery men he'd spoken with a couple of days before and walked over to where they were looking out over the British line.

None of them were speaking, so James asked, "Are the French cannon having any effect at all on the enemy, aside from keeping them from sleeping, too?"

One of the artillery men glanced over with disdain in his expression and approached James. "What, can't you sleep through a little exercise of the big guns? My companions and I haven't been troubled at all." He grinned and continued, "As to whether the French guns have done us any good, we were just trying to judge that for ourselves."

He pointed to an area of higher ground just visible above the tangled branches of the abattis. "We think the British have gun emplacements there, there, and there, in addition to what they have on the other side of town, and what those Ethiopian troops found here."

His finger moved along the British line as he spoke, but James was momentarily confused by the comment about "Ethiopian" troops.

"Do you mean the regiment from Saint-Domingue, consisting of free negroes?"

"Aye, Saint-Domingue, Ethiopian, whatever they choose to call themselves. The blackbirds who got themselves chopped to mincemeat a fortnight ago."

The artillery man seemed amused at his own comment, and it was all James could do to swallow his anger at his dismissive tone.

"Yes, I was there," he bit out, "and tended to their wounded and dead. They were led into the slaughter by an officer who had found his courage in a bottle, and 'tis none of their fault that he should have turned out to be so inept."

"As you say," the other man said, placidly. Dismissing James' angry tone with a calming gesture, he continued his analysis. "In any event, we should like to see those emplacements struck by our French friends, but the enemy have located them with great cunning, what with the screen they've erected before their earthworks, and the redoubts they managed to erect before our arrival."

He frowned and spoke to another of the artillery soldiers, "Justin, do you think we could do better than these French gun crews at overcoming the advantages of terrain and planning that the British have over us?"

Justin sucked air thoughtfully between his teeth. "I don't think so, no. Now that they have sobered up, those French crews seem to be just about as good as our best, and maybe even a touch better. Naturally, I would never permit one of my crews to assume the duties of firing a cannon were they not as sober as General Lincoln, but different troops have different practices."

James had heard others refer to their general's peculiar avoidance of both strong drink and strong words, but he was amused to hear it used to qualify the suitability for duty of an artillery crew.

The first man James had been speaking with nodded, and turned to him to explain, "Those big guns are nothing to play at unless every man on the crew is at his best. A whole lot of your own men can wind up blown to bits and scattered to the four horizons in an awful hurry if any one of them makes a mistake."

He ticked off the possibilities on his fingers. "If someone errs in handling the charge before it's in place in the gun, *boom*. Everyone dies. Misjudge how warm the barrel has gotten, and *boom*, the whole crew is ripped apart. Tamp down the charge too enthusiastically, so it can't send the ball where it needs to go, and the barrel can still explode. *Boom*, another crew gone."

He shook his head. "That's not even counting the ways a man can kill just himself. If the powder isn't kept dry, and fails to ignite when the gun is touched off, then someone needs to fish the bad charge out. Misjudge that, or worse, set it off in the attempt, and you'll be on your way to meet Saint Peter at the gates to heaven before you even know what hit you."

He shrugged. "I even saw a fellow not paying close enough attention to where the crew was in the firing sequence, and he contrived to put his face in front of the muzzle as the charge was lit. We never did find his head."

James shuddered in spite of himself. "How is it, then, that the French crews have managed to avoid disaster?"

The artillery man shrugged. "Fortune smiles on fools as often as on knaves."

He laughed and returned his attention to the British lines. "In any event, our enemies have had some good luck in the terrain, and some good leadership in their disposition and use of the landscape. We will need to trust in the advantage of overwhelming numbers to reduce theirs and bring them to terms in the end, so that we can quit this miserable place for a drier and more congenial field of battle."

James frowned. "Having witnessed at close range the effectiveness of the British grapeshot on troops who strayed within their range, I have no great desire to fling myself within reach of their guns. Do you suppose there are places along their works that lie outside of the range of their cannon?"

"Not too likely, given the skill with which their defenses seem to be arrayed," the soldier answered. "I have heard some say that the hill just here" — he led James a short distance to a spot where they could see where the road from Augusta entered the town, and pointed to it — "offers us the best approach to the town, but the defenders will have noted that, as well."

James answered sourly, "So there is little doubt that those abattis up behind the brow of the hill conceal gun batteries, just waiting to slice us to ribbons, should we try that path."

"Just so," the man answered. "I do not know the generals' minds, but if I were planning the assault, I should think some other target would be better to preserve our strength . . . but doing so to no purpose for the advancement of the cause is also a useless gesture."

The artillery man frowned, looking out over the massed American and French troops in their encampments. "The best way to make use of our advantage in numbers is to be willing to use those numbers, which will mean losing some in the effort."

James grimaced. "It is all well and good for a campside general to speak so casually of expending anonymous 'numbers,' but every one of those numbers has a face, a name, and a home he is eager to return to some day."

The artillery soldier nodded agreement. "Aye, and that is why I will never be aught but a campside general. I would shudder to issue the orders that would throw men to their certain deaths, even if I should be assured that it would result in our national liberation. No, I do not envy those generals their responsibilities."

"Nor will they envy us ours, when that day comes, and we are among the men who may be ordered to die for the cause."

The man's face was touched with the briefest of smiles. "No, I doubt that they will, but even the highest general may be brought low by a musket ball well-aimed. Death comes for us all, by and by."

He paused, and added in a more sober and thoughtful tone, "I would rather sleep in a grave by the site of a battle won, than in my own bed safe at home, only to read of the heroic sacrifices of other men."

James thought about what his father's reaction had been to his enlistment. He wondered idly if any of the men on the other side of the British line were Loyalists, and if so, whether any might be kin.

He knew that his parents would just as soon have him sleeping at home, but it would have been hard indeed to hear news of neighbors undertaking this duty to American independence, and then to have returned to his comfortable and warm bed.

He shook his head to dispel the thought, and gave the soldier a brief, tight half-smile. "Well, I should prefer most of all to survive the day, and to return home after having won the field, with stories of great accomplishments and brave deeds to share."

"Even if they are the accomplishments and deeds of others, eh? The girls need not know which soldier performed the deeds you describe, so long as they are thrilling enough." The artillery man chuckled at his own witticism, but James shook his head, smiling.

"Nay, I would rather take credit for my own modest contributions than claim the glory earned by another man, even if there were no chance that someone might smoke me out."

The other soldier clapped him on the back. "Well, then, you are a better man than I, my friend. Alas, we should attend to our duties, and stop sharing gossip and speculation about matters that are far beyond our ken, never mind control."

"Aye, I am supposed to be back in my camp, preparing more cartridges for the battle to come."

"Best you get to it, then. Until we speak again — and may good fortune continue to smile upon you."

"I hope that you stay safe, as well."

The man waved farewell to James, and wandered back over to where his friends were still observing the French gunnery.

James continued on his way to camp, where men were sitting on whatever stools and chairs they could find or improvise, carefully preparing round after round of cartridges to speed their loading in battle.

One could, of course, measure out the powder directly from a horn into the muzzle of a musket, pack down a wad atop it, and tamp the ball over that before priming, cocking, and firing, but in the middle of a battle, there was no time for that kind of slow, deliberate loading.

So they prepared cartridges, measuring the powder and shot into paper, and twisting the end to secure it, and then dropping each one into a cartridge bag, where it was nestled into a hole drilled into the wooden insert.

When the time came, the cartridge would be pulled out, the end torn off with one's teeth, and the measured powder charge poured into the muzzle. The paper of the cartridge served as the wadding, and it was a well-graven, practiced series of motions to prime, charge, load, cock, and fire by this method, enabling troops to pour ammunition into the ranks of their enemies at a far higher rate of fire than was otherwise possible.

All of those advantages aside, preparing cartridges was one of James' least favorite ways to pass an afternoon. The work was exacting and repetitive, and it only served to remind him that his officers expected violence was imminent.

He felt certain that soldiers on the other side of the line were doing likewise, and this did nothing at all to soothe his nerves — although it did serve to encourage care and speed in the work itself.

It was near to supper time when James finally finished preparing his allotment of cartridges, and his hands ached from the labor. Even more, his eyes burned from focusing at such close range for all those hours, and even his back was stiff from hunching over to protect the powder from wind and damp.

He was grateful indeed to collapse onto his bedroll that evening, and, despite the continued booming of the French cannon, sleep claimed him solidly all night.

Chapter II

Fog clung to the ground nearly as tenaciously as the mud of the swamp clung to James' boots. He was happy enough that he had not been assigned to the force approaching the hill that the artillery soldier had pointed out some days earlier, but being a part of the diversionary attack on the eastern edge of the town was hardly any more comfortable.

His sergeant had impressed upon the entire troop the importance of utter silence. Gathering them close around a banked cooking fire, he'd hissed into the pre-dawn darkness, "Any man who so much as coughs, I'll push you into the swamp myself and hold you down until the bubbles stop. The enemy must have no warning whatever until we open fire on their positions. Do I make myself perfectly clear?"

A quiet mumble of agreement seemed to satisfy him, and he continued. "You lot are not considered skilled enough for the main attack, but you have an opportunity to redeem yourselves by drawing defenders off that little rise by the Augusta road that the residents hereabouts call Spring Hill, where most of our force will be concentrated."

James was unsurprised by their assignment, but others seemed to have anticipated some other plan, and a low murmur passed through them.

The sergeant hissed, "Silence all around. I am not yet

finished. If we can convince them that we are mounting the main attack, the British will send their forces to meet us. Once that happens, we are to retreat with all due haste, and draw them yet further away from the *real* main attack."

He looked around at the troops he could see, and shook his head in a show of disgust. "It's a pity I've been burdened with such poor recruits, but perhaps you will surprise me and comport yourselves with some distinction. We'll be guided by a local farmer who's been recruited to show us the best paths through the swamp, and we may hope that in their haste to follow us, and without such a local guide, the British will be mired down while we fly to safety."

He grimaced. "If not, well . . . we will stand and fight for as long as we are able, if only to engage what forces of the enemy whose attention we can command."

Now that they were where they had been directed to go, James felt even less certain about his prospects of seeing the sun rise, never mind witnessing its setting this evening.

The British seemed to be stirring within their positions — James could hear snatches of the horrid, eerie music of the Scots pipers drifting out from over the town. He shuddered, hoping that those troops were only drilling for some inscrutable purpose in the dark of the night.

The cessation of the French artillery bombardment had, without a doubt, alerted the British to the coming attack, but would they know what form it would take?

He remembered the words of the artillery soldier, who had praised the skill the enemy had shown in placing its cannon. It seemed likely that the same principles would be employed in placing their troops to receive the expected allied attack.

Once again, despite what felt like dismal prospects for the survival of those assigned to undertake the feint, James was glad not to be a part of the main force. He thought about Prevard, Legrand, and the rest of his friends among the French forces, and silently wished them well as the minutes slipped past.

Finally, the order he'd anticipated for what seemed like hours was passed along the line in a hoarse whisper. "Prime and load!"

He unslung his musket and opened the priming pan, trying to coordinate his movements with those of the man next to him in the dim light of the coming morning.

Even without the command being spoken aloud, he heard inside his head, "Handle - cartridge!"

He pulled a cartridge from his bag and tore off the top with his teeth, sliding his thumb over the open end as he did so.

On the count, he chanted silently to himself, "Prime!"

He dropped a pinch of powder into the pan, and closed the frizzen to hold it in.

He reached the call of "Bout!" in his mind, and swung the musket about to point its muzzle skyward, with the wooden stock resting on the ground beside his foot, and poured the rest of the charge down the barrel, followed by the paper and ball of the cartridge.

He caught himself chanting under his breath now, and chastised himself.

"Draw - ramrods!"

The ramrod slid smoothly out of its hoops, and he set its end into the top of the barrel. He heard the man to his left answer in time with the count, just barely audible.

"Ram - down the cartridge!"

Even without the sergeant shouting the orders, he could hear the men around him moving in reasonably good synchronization. He drove the ball and wadding down the barrel and gave it two careful tamps, as he'd drilled over and over again.

"Return - ramrods!"

None spoke aloud now, even under their breaths. He slid the ramrod back into its place under the barrel, so that it would be exactly where he expected it when he needed to fire again.

"Make - ready!"

He brought his gun back up to his chest, holding it in position to wait for the sergeant's actual call down the line.

"Present - arms!"

The sergeant was no longer trying to be silent, but used his voice at full volume now to ensure that his troops were, in fact, operating as one.

James brought the stock of his gun up to his shoulder, and sighted down the barrel, aiming at the spark of a watchman's fire that he could glimpse fitfully dancing under its column of smoke, just above the fog that enveloped the ground beneath the town.

"And - fire!"

James' finger tensed over his trigger, and he heard the flint snap against the striker, the malignant hiss of the priming charge catching, and then felt, rather than heard, the roar and kick of his musket against his shoulder, among the din of all the others surrounding him.

He immediately drew the gun around to the prime and load position, and pursed his lips to blow out the open pan and ensure that no sparks remained, before the command echoed again in the smoke and fog, "Prime and load!"

An eternity later, after firing several volleys as a relatively unified force, the first return fire came back from the defenders. James saw the fog light up, with the coordinated fire from the enemy, and a moment later, heard the first screams of pain from those among his detail who had been hit.

He did not let it interrupt his own smooth flow of movement as he continued through the drill of loading and readying his gun to return fire yet again.

"And - fire!"

All other noise disappeared in the roar of musketry around him. As that sound faded, though, the deeper boom of terrible cannon fire rippled from the distance, and James could almost imagine that he heard answering cries from French voices in the darkness.

"Prime and load!"

His practiced movements continued without conscious thought, and James felt as though he were watching some stranger operate his arms and hands in a strange sort of puppetry.

"And - fire!"

Again, an answering flash of musketry lit up the heights before them. The man to James' right fell heavily into the muck, without uttering so much as a sigh.

"Ad - vance!"

James struggled to pull his feet free of the swampy ground, then moved forward until he heard the sergeant's strong voice call out over the pop of musketry near and far, and the deeper thunder of cannon, "Form your lines!"

James was relieved to find that they had gained slightly

more solid ground under foot as he formed up with the men to either side of him, closing the gap left by the one who had fallen.

After a moment came the call once again, "Prime and load!"

The light of dawn was slowly rising now, but the fog and smoke still concealed the enemy lines nearly as well as had the dark of night. If anything, there was less to guide his aim now, without the guard's campfire to focus on.

Another flash of enemy musket fire marked their location, though, so he was ready for the call, "Present - arms!" It didn't sound as though anyone had been struck by the enemy's most recent volley, and the command to fire followed in another moment.

As James continued to prime, load, tamp, aim, and fire, over and over again, he found that his mind wandered, as though his full attention was no longer needed while he completed these merely mechanical operations.

The thunder and crackle of the battle on the far side of town continued unabated, and he wondered what that portended for success of the attack. Shouldn't they have been able to overwhelm the enemy's cannon by now?

Cannon boomed from a new quarter — was that one of the British ships on the river, now joining in? — and James watched another man further down the line topple to the soggy ground with an agonized shout, thrashing for a moment before falling still.

Now, there was musket fire coming from somewhere closer by. James was unsurprised to hear the sergeant shout, "Fall back! Retreat in good order, until I give you the command to stand and fire again."

He glanced at the man beside him, and saw the indecision in his eyes. James offered him a quick smile of assurance, before turning on his heel and, starting with a deliberate, measured step back toward the swamp.

The other soldier followed his lead, and the retreat was, overall, largely orderly — up until the moment another volley of musket fire sounded from behind them, and the man James had reassured screamed and fell to one knee, clutching at a fresh wound in his thigh.

At that, the retreat turned into a general sprint, despite the sergeant's shouted commands. As he hit the swampy ground again, James stumbled over the unmoving corpse of one of the first men to fall. He caught himself, recovering to slog through the muck, until he and those around him emerged into the sparse woods on the other side, where they broke into a trot toward the designated rallying point.

The sergeant's voice had been silenced before they made it out of the swamp, his shouts to form up and "Prime and load" having been cut off by another volley from the enemy pursuers.

His interrupted last order was ignored by all, and the remaining men broke into an open run as they scrambled to get beyond the reach of the British musketry.

Despite his personal survival, as he stopped and caught his breath, James felt as though his detail's part in the attack on the British had been nothing short of a disaster. Joining the line of troops streaming back toward the rendezvous they'd been instructed to attempt, he hoped that the main attack was going better.

When they reached the old Jewish burying-ground on the far side of the town, a, young, scared-looking French officer was going down the line of men, looking over each one, and gesturing for most of them to form up.

James was wearily preparing to join the formation when the French officer shook his head and waved him over toward where a medic was treating the wounded.

James shot the man a questioning look, and the officer impatiently pointed to the flank of his jacket.

James was shocked to glance down and find that it was soaked through with blood, and even more amazed to realize that it was his own.

Reaching down, he found a neat hole in the back of the jacket, just under his ribs, and understood in a rush that the stitch in his side wasn't from running.

He turned toward the medic, and was only mildly surprised to see Perrault's familiar face.

The French doctor raised his eyebrows in simultaneous recognition, and said, briskly, "Get your top off, so that we can see what your wounds are."

Having obediently stripped off his jacket and shirt, James quickly grew very chilly, as fog and smoke mingled to conceal the departing troops the French officer had assembled.

Perrault warned, "This is going to hurt like the very devil, but it will make what I must do next hurt somewhat less." James could smell the sharp reek of rum almost at the same instant that it flowed over his open flesh, and it was all he could do to stifle the shout that wanted to erupt from his throat. He settled for uttering a low moan, but he suppressed even that as quickly as he could.

He tried to take his mind off of the sharp pains and tugs of the medic's probing fingers and then, his hurried needle, by attempting to discern how the battle was proceeding. He wasn't in a good vantage point to see anything of it, but he could hear the ongoing crack and pop of musketry, occasionally punctuated with the deeper boom of cannon.

He thought, too, that he could hear an occasional snatch of shouted commands, and more chillingly, the screams of wounded men, but it was hard to know how much of either was being supplied by his imagination.

In short order, the medic said, brusquely, "You'll live, I think, if any of us do. Get dressed and take what time you need to recover yourself. I've no doubt that another draft of men will be called up to the line soon enough."

"I wasn't hurt badly, then?"

"Nay." Perrault held up a lead ball smeared with blood, and offered it to James, who took it and examined it with curious detachment.

The medic continued, "Most of its momentum was spent by the time it reached you, and your jacket further slowed it. The thing hardly more than scratched you, but the wound was wide enough to merit sewing up."

He looked James over. "You'll be more sore tomorrow than you are today, by a long way, but you should remain fit for whatever duty there may be."

James kept the musket ball in his hand as he pulled on his shirt and tucked it roughly into his breeches. As he stretched to pull his jacket on over his arm, he winced, feeling now where he'd been shot. He dropped the ball into the pocket of his jacket, with a plan to arrange to have it drilled later for a lucky necklace.

On any other day, it could have lodged somewhere far more vital, and left him lying somewhere in the muck with his sergeant.

A sudden roar of concentrated cannon fire caused both men's heads to jerk toward the battlefield. A few troops could be seen rushing around in the smoke, but there seemed to be nothing resembling an organized effort, until a knot of horsemen came back away from the town, followed shortly by French and American troops withdrawing from the line.

The medic said, under his breath, "*Merde*," and turned to gather up his equipment. "I will put you to work myself. We will need to go gather up the wounded. The battle is lost."

Chapter 12

"We have but four hours to collect our dead and bring the wounded back to camp for treatment," Doctor Perrault was saying, but James could hardly focus on the man's words.

Before the British redoubts, men were impaled on the sharpened stakes that remained of the abattis for dozens of yards in both directions. But that was only the start of the horrors that would haunt James for the rest of his days.

The gap where the stakes and brambles had been cleared revealed a broad ditch strewn with the mortal remains of what had to have been hundreds more French and American soldiers.

Some were identifiable as human corpses, but many had been so torn apart by grapeshot and cannon balls that they were little more than scattered pieces of meat.

In addition to the heavy smell of brimstone, the charnel stench of blood and torn flesh was enough to raise James' gorge, and Perrault waited with visible impatience as James' stomach heaved out what little it contained from his breakfast.

A few men milled around the ditch aimlessly, and the medic pressed each one into service as they came within range of his voice. James was shocked and relieved to see that one of these was Claude, but he could discern at a glance that the man was in a terrible state.

He hurried to his friend's side, though he recoiled when he

saw that Claude clutched another man's hand — only the hand.

Claude was staring blankly down at his burden, the tears pouring from his eyes leaving trails — the only clean spots on his face.

James gently prompted, "Claude?" He put an arm around the man's shoulder, and guiding him away from the reckless carnage of the ditch.

The French soldier slowly looked up. In a plaintive and terrible voice, he moaned "*Henri. C'est Henri.*" He lifted the hand to show it to James, and his face screwed up in overwhelming grief, his shoulders shaking with uncontrollable weeping.

He added something else in French, but all that James could make out in the broken and unintelligible words was Henri's name, again.

He pulled Claude into his arms and held the tall soldier as his frame was racked with the sort of sobs that leave a man's throat raw, and his mind in pieces.

James heard Doctor Perrault call to him, and carefully extricated his friend from his embrace. Catching Perrault's eye, he lifted one finger to ask for just a moment longer. The doctor shook his head impatiently, but waved a hand in acknowledgment.

James turned back to Claude. Chewing his lip to control his own grief and horror, he said, urgently, "Claude. Henri must be buried." He gestured at the hand, and then pantomimed digging.

Claude's eyes filled again, but he nodded, before his face collapsed once more into cries of soul-rending pain. Taking his friend by the arm, James guided him in the direction of Perrault.

When they reached the doctor, James said quietly, "My friend has lost a dear companion, and he carries what he could find of the man's remains. Will you explain to him what must be done, and what more you need of him?"

Perrault looked at Claude's face, and his expression softened when he saw the burden in the soldier's hand. The doctor spoke in a gentle tone, and the other man nodded miserably, answering with halting, hoarse words.

The doctor gestured around them and then up to the British guns, readily visible from where they stood. He said something further and reached out his hand. Reluctantly, slowly, Claude yielded Henri's hand over to the doctor.

Perrault accepted it, cupping it in his palms and closing the dead man's fingers gently with his own. After placing the hand reverently into the horse-drawn wagon where the dead were being gathered, he made one last remark to Claude.

The tall man's face once again crumpled into raw, unfiltered anguish, and he turned to James, clutching at the American as though to keep from drowning in the overwhelming emotions he was suffering.

James wrapped a comforting arm around the man until Doctor Perrault said, quietly, "I think that this man will be of little use to us here. I will send him back to the encampment while we finish our awful work."

James nodded and released Claude. Perrault told the heartbroken man to depart, and James watched him go, unsurprised to discover that he was weeping himself.

As Claude stumbled away, James wondered whether Prevard had survived the day, but tossed his head to dispel that gloomy question. There was loss enough surrounding him without wondering at the possibility of more.

He stooped and picked up a man's leg and put it on the cart, and then he and Perrault wordlessly bent at either end of a more intact corpse to add it to the growing pile. He paused long enough to close the dead man's sightless eyes, then returned to the carnage around him to retrieve the next victim of the British grapeshot.

"Looks like an officer here," he remarked, pointing at the epaulet on the shoulder of a headless, limbless trunk.

Perrault scowled. "No way to know which one he was. Some French lieutenant — one of dozens, and I only knew a handful. I have never learned enough to know the buttons of one regiment's coats from another. Let's go ahead and put this poor fellow in with the others."

They hoisted the torso up onto the wagon and proceeded to the next torn and bloody heap.

When they had gathered what they could from it, Perrault looked about and proclaimed, "There are no more living souls here at all."

He grimaced and gestured back toward the French encampment. "My patients need me more than these unfortunates. I will send a detail out to help you finish the job, and some more wagons, as well."

The rest of the time permitted by the terms imposed by the victors passed in this morbid manner, with wounded soldiers gathering up the scraps of their unlucky compatriots that still laid before the gates of this now decisively British town.

When they had done their best to collect enough of each man to give him a decent burial, they had the drovers on each wagon turn their grim loads around and bring them back to the places hastily designated as grave sites outside of town for interment and prayer. James swallowed hard as he noticed the broad trail of blood in the soil that had traced out the path of the wagon as it drew away.

Behind the main French encampment, men were already engaged in opening a gaping scar in the muck to receive the mortal remains of their fellow soldiers. James watched, drained of all emotion, as one wagon after another tipped out its wretched cargo.

Each occasion when James saw a familiar face among the dead was a fresh shock, but none of them were granted even a moment of individual attention, in the tumble and splash of fresh bodies and other parts into the muddy mass grave.

A few officers who could be identified were accorded individual graves, and even those were shallow, half-hearted affairs. All the rest went into a single long wound torn into the soil of this place, a jumble of limbs and flesh that nearly filled it to the top.

As the last of the wagons bumped away over the uneven ground, weary men with shovels closed in around the gaping maw of the mass grave. One shovel full at a time, they covered their former companions with sandy soil, which drank up the blood thirstily as it settled over what was left of the proud American and French soldiers.

James felt his stomach roil again at the sight, and he turned away, trudging back to his company's area in the American encampment. There, he found a few of the men sitting around the fire pit, though nobody had bothered to stoke up the cooking fire.

James found a seat and settled into it, staring into the ashes as though they might hold some meaning beyond commemorating the wood spent to heat up supper the night before. How many men had eaten their last meal from the cooking pots that now hung loosely over the pit?

He shook his head, dismissing the thought.

The lieutenant, his uniform spattered with ichor and a fresh bandage wrapped around his calf, limped in from between the tents and sat down heavily on the ground, his eyes as dead as James thought his own must be. At the sight of the officer's bandage, James' wound, which he had nearly forgotten about, began to throb in sympathy.

Finally, someone spoke up, asking the lieutenant, "Do you reckon we're done for here?"

The officer didn't seem to hear at first, his flat gaze trapped on the side of his own boot. After a long moment, he looked up to see who had spoken, and his head turned slowly, almost aimlessly, from side to side.

When he answered, his voice was barely more than a hoarse whisper. "No, sir, I don't reckon we are at that." He took a deep breath, appearing to be carefully considering what to say next. "We will do our duty here, for so long as the generals command it, or until the last man of our company has been extinguished from this earth."

The lieutenant's gaze slowly wandered around the encampment, before settling on a vision that only he could see, on the far side of their tents. "When the drums and fifes call to us, when the cannon lure us forth, we will answer."

His voice grew stronger. "When the enemy's guns howl for our blood, and their bayonets glint in the light of the sunrise, awaiting our throats, we will advance as we are called upon to do."

Finally, his eyes steadied, and he looked at the men gathered around the cooking pit, meeting their stares one by one. "We have been granted by the great Author of this world the privilege of standing upright to throw off the yoke of tyranny imposed by those who would use the debased tools of this world to reduce us to permanent servitude. That privilege comes at a terrible price, and by God, we have paid it this day."

Some of the men stirred uncomfortably, their faces belying their concern as to the lieutenant's state of mind, but he did not take notice.

Instead, he barreled on, "The coin of the realm of liberty is the blood and bodies of patriots, and we have spent that coin freely today — but that only means that when we enjoy the fruits of that purchase, they will be all the sweeter!"

The officer stood and fixed James with a fierce expression, his eyes burning with a special madness. He roared now, "When we are again offered the chance to add to the price paid for this nation's independence from the tyrant king, we should be glad that we have been selected for that rare opportunity. Our posterity will remember our names, each and every one, and will engrave them upon their hearts in celebration forever!"

His finger still lifted to the sky in punctuation, his expression transformed suddenly to one of puzzlement, before he toppled to the ground face-first, where he then lay, silenced and still.

Chapter 13

The French were abandoning them here. Of this, the American forces had no doubt, as they watched their erstwhile allies carefully fold up their tents and load them onto wagons for transport to the waiting ships of the squadron that had brought them to Savannah.

What started as angry mutters turned into open jeers as the French regiments formed up and started to march for the anchorage where their transports stood. James stood silent as some of the members of his reduced company joined in on the derisive shouts directed at the passing column of soldiers.

He was frankly surprised at how quickly the mood of the American troops had shifted, and he wondered how they could have forgotten so soon how many of their allies lay in the ground behind them, never to make the return trip home.

Those now shouting insults had been happy enough to let the French forces lead the charge up Spring Hill and dash themselves against the walls of the British fortifications. It soured James' stomach to hear them so abused now.

He was not the only one to feel that way. Their new lieutenant came tearing into the encampment and shouted orders for the company to fall into formation, his tone brooking no argument.

Once everyone was standing silent before him, he lit into

them, his tone furious.

"Do you not know that their commanding general himself was shot three times in the attempt to take this town? Why, the man was left for dead before the gates at Spring Hill, and it was only through the heroic efforts of his officers that he was recovered so he might return to the field another time."

He glared up and down the line, and James was heartened to see some abashed-looking faces among those who'd been the loudest voices of criticism.

Their lieutenant continued, "They do not owe you lot an explanation, but I will pass it along regardless. Their ships cannot bear the weather of the advanced season, and indeed, their commanders risked losing all in their determination to see this town retaken."

He gestured in the direction of the town, again concealed behind the abattis that James knew all too well was a vicious trap for any would-be attacker. "If you want to be angry, save your rage for the enemy who employed every form of barbarism ever imagined on a battlefield to lay our allies low. They ought to be the target of your fury, not these men who fought beside you, and whose blood soaks the ground along with yours."

He shook his head, his own fury apparently spent, leaving behind only sadness and disappointment. "I know your frustration well, my friends. I had hoped that we might make another attempt at redeeming the town of Savannah from the enemy's clutches. But that was not to be, and though we may have lost the day, there are other battles to fight, and the larger contest with the British is yet undecided."

He glanced over at the French soldiers, still passing in their hundreds on the way to their ships. "In the meantime, the only salute I want to see you offering our allies, our brothers in blood, on this field of battle is one of gratitude and respect. They have earned both."

He turned away, calling out over his shoulder, "Dismissed. As you were."

The men fell out of formation, and small knots of soldiers quietly considered their officer's words.

James drifted toward one group, and heard a man say, "The lieutenant isn't entirely wrong, but it still rankles to see the French sail away, while we must either stand and try to hold the siege ourselves, or else march back up the road and wait to be thrown onto another blood-soaked field."

Another man echoed the lieutenant's words. "They've overstayed their safe departure, as it is. And without them having come here in the first place, we should never have had a chance to even attempt to eject the British."

He shrugged, and concluded, "Having made the effort, and at great cost to themselves, it seems ungracious to begrudge them their safe passage away from here."

For his own part, James was sad to see the French leave, if only because he felt that he had found truer friends among their ranks than among the American forces. He despaired of seeing Prevard or even Claude again, though. He knew not whether Prevard was in the grave behind their camp, and the last time he'd seen Claude, the man had been too shattered at his companion's loss to even walk a straight line.

Watching the column passing by, he spotted Doctor Perrault supporting a wounded soldier as both struggled to keep up with their regiment. James hurried over to offer assistance, and to say his farewells to the medical man.

He slipped the injured soldier's arm over his shoulder, and almost without acknowledging the fellow who he now helped bear, said to Perrault, "We will sorely miss your company, sir."

He stifled a gasp as more of the soldier's weight fell onto his shoulder, pulling at the stitches in his swollen wound.

Perrault looked haggard and unkempt, but with as much gallantry as he could muster, he replied, "And I will miss your assistance, Private. Not many could stomach the work you helped me with, and if I had any contact with the American medical service, I would gladly commend you to their ranks."

James ducked his head at the praise, but said, "I appreciate that, sir, but I think I have had my fill of picking up bits and pieces of fallen men, or else trying to hold together the ones who still breathe and cry out."

Perrault gave him a half-smile. "It does seem as though that is most of what you and I have done together, doesn't it? But I will tell you that there is no small satisfaction in being able to rescue a man from the very brink of the hereafter, and deliver him safely to his loving home."

He nodded at the soldier now nearly suspended by his arms across their shoulders. "Take Private Michaud, here."

The man between them stirred, looking up for a moment at the mention of his name, but seemed to find the effort of holding his head up to be too much, as he let it fall to his chest again.

"Without my help, that leg would have easily been the end of him. Since he has no English, I can tell you freely that it may yet be, but at least I can bring him to live for as long as he can aboard a ship aiming to bring him home. And he's a lucky one for that."

The doctor motioned with his chin toward the remaining French encampment. "I've had to leave a large number of men who are too badly hurt to bring aboard yet. But do not worry. So as not to burden your forces, the generals have assigned a detachment of the *Chasseurs-Volontaires* to bring them along with your regiments to wherever you are going next."

James' eyebrows shot up. "Do you know whether my friends may be among those who are staying?"

Perrault pursed his lips in thought. "Do you mean that unfortunate corporal, who discovered the remains of his companion, and was so wrought up by the man's death that I had to send him from the battlefield?"

"Yes, he is one of those whom I know best among your number."

The medical man nodded. "I do believe he is staying behind, though I cannot recall in all honesty whether it is as a patient or as an escort to our wounded."

James bit the inside of his lip to hold back the tears that threatened to spring to his eyes. "I shall endeavor to assist him, then, in whichever capacity he may be here. He served quite closely with a Corporal Prevard. Do you know that man?"

Perrault shook his head. "No, I do not come to know very many by name. They are more usually known to me by their injuries. This fellow is the shattered kneecap, for example, and your friend I know only as the lost nerve."

He shrugged under the wounded soldier's arm. "It is easier for me to do for them what I must do *without* names, so I do not think of them as men with mothers and brothers and wives. And if I cannot avoid coming to know their names, I make no effort to remember them for any longer than it takes to get their attention."

His eyes took on a distant expression, and he added, quietly, "I prefer, too, that I do not remember the names of the men whose lives I cannot preserve." He looked over at James. "This work is difficult enough without having a list of those whose names haunt me, in addition to their injuries."

James nodded, not really knowing how to reply to this confession. It seemed an odd way to encourage him to consider taking up the profession himself — if that had even been the doctor's intention.

They neared the edge of the clearing around the town, and the doctor said, "You ought not go much further."

He shot James a quick half-smile. "Indeed, you should not have even come out to help, *monsieur* graze wound. I will have someone from our own number help me get this kneecap onto the ship."

He shifted the soldier's weight back onto himself. "I wish you good fortune in finding your friends, and will pray that a just God will keep and preserve you through the days to come."

He called out in French to one of the soldiers marching in the column, and as the man he'd summoned took Private Michaud's arm over his own shoulder, James turned fully to face the doctor.

"I will likewise remember you in my prayers, sir, and I thank you for the care you have given to me. I do not expect that our paths will cross again in this world, but I will recall your name for all of my days."

Doctor Perrault acknowledged James with a deep, respectful incline of his head. Without another word, he turned away and continued alongside the column of French troops, supporting his side of the man with the broken knee and trudging out of sight up the road toward his ship.

Chapter 14

James winced as he stretched to unfasten one of the walls of his tent in preparation to march for the relief of Charles-Town, up the coast in South-Carolina.

It seemed to him that it ought to be an occasion of relief, even joy, but he found that he was unaccountably sad to help his messmates dismantle the canvas shelter.

His wound was healing up well, at least, free of the angry swelling and infection that too often followed an injury of that nature. He'd clipped the knot off of one end of the thread that Doctor Perrault had used to close the wound and carefully, painfully, drawn it out the prior day.

All around him, men called to one another as they coordinated their efforts, but the mood around the encampment was subdued. There were all too many chests set aside, their owners dead or having deserted, and everyone was keenly aware of the long, low mound behind the town.

As the tent came down, James noticed that it left an elaborate tracery of paths on the ground around and within it marking the passage of his own feet and many others' as they'd moved with purpose from duty to desperation to death.

His own mood was scarcely brightened by having found Claude among the French forces. Other than clasping the man's hand to express his joy at finding him unhurt and in good health, there was little he could do to communicate with him, absent the services of Thomas or Corporal Prevard.

The Negro soldier still bore an all-encompassing air of grief, and even when he did venture a few brief comments in French, his voice was small and hopeless-sounding.

James had asked him, speaking slowly and emphasizing each word as though it would somehow enable Claude to understand the English, "Do you know where Corporal Prevard is?"

Claude had answered in French, shaking his head. The only words that James could understand were "*Non*," and Prevard's name. But he could not determine whether Claude was telling him that the other corporal was lost, dead, departed, or simply that he had no idea of his fate.

Folding and rolling up the rain-spattered canvas of his tent alongside Patrick, James reflected that the other man would probably have no kind words for his preoccupation with his French friends' fates.

Since he'd broken Patrick's face, they had exchanged no more than a dozen words.

Even now, they worked in silence as they prepared the tent for storage, mindlessly following the instructions drilled into them what seemed like a lifetime ago.

Holding up the finished tent roll while the other man lashed it tightly with hempen rope, James looked around absently at the men around him who were similarly occupied.

"There," Patrick grunted, tying off the last rope. He turned away, leaving James to hoist the canvas onto his shoulder with another wince and deliver it to the baggage wagon.

The soldier in charge of securing the load scowled at him,

though it seemed more out of habit than out of any particular irritation with James' delivery.

James asked, "Do you need me to move that somewhere else on the wagon?"

The drover looked over the load and shook his head. "Makes no difference at this point. We have barely enough horses to haul all of this, and the roads have gotten no better since we came this way. I don't see how we're going to manage all the way to Charleston without we have got some relief somewhere along the way."

James nodded sympathetically. "Don't you expect we'll meet up with some supporters somewhere short of the city, who will be happy enough to help us make our way to its defense?"

The soldier shrugged, reminding James for a moment of Thomas and his great, expressive shrugs. "'Tis hard to say, friend. They should see it as being in their self-interest, but how likely is a defeated army to find enthusiastic help in its next undertaking?"

James frowned, thinking about this. Finally, he asked, "Do you truly believe we are seen as nothing more than a defeated army? I should think that there is at least some sentiment in our favor, after we have given so freely of our blood and toil in the service of American independence."

The soldier scoffed, "Effort is not what most people care about. Only results get entered into their account books, and our results here were as awful as anyone could ever have guessed. How many hundreds did we bury or otherwise leave behind? How many hundreds more limp along with us, and will never again be fit for duty?"

He waved a frustrated, dismissive hand back toward the

town. "And for what? Some little port town in the middle of nowhere, whose people probably number fewer than the forces gathered here to contest its fate. Why, I doubt that so much blood was spilled at Bunker Hill, and that contest was at least over a full-sized city."

He spat, carefully aiming away from James. "We failed to demonstrate that we could fight well alongside our allies, we exposed to the enemy the weakness of our leadership, and we threw away some three companies' worth of men in the process."

James raised a hand to quiet the soldier, who let him interject, "Not every military loss is a failure, friend. You mentioned Bunker Hill, which ended in a rout of our armies — yet it rallies men to our cause to this day."

He gestured in the direction of the hurt and sick camp. "The French depart still allies with us, and further, continue to supply us with troops to help tend to the wounded. Naturally, we should all prefer to arrive covered in glory and bearing the standards of our defeated enemies, but we cannot overlook the fact that we will nonetheless be arriving, and that our arms and men will be welcome."

Another man came and deposited his rolled tent on the wagon, turned away without comment, and trudged back towards the encampment.

The soldier at the wagon frowned at first, but then a reluctant smile crept over his face. "You have a positive gift for finding some bright jot in a dark frame, and amplifying that, while doing your best to look away from the rest. I am not certain whether that is a blessing or a curse, but I suppose I will take it to heart today."

Offering his hand, he said. "I am Paul Oaker, of Harden's South-Carolina, and you?"

James accepted the handshake. "James Hatch, of Huger's Continental."

"'Tis a pleasure to make your acquaintance, James." The man's smile was more unguarded now, and James couldn't help but return it.

"Likewise, Paul. Where are you originally from?"

"Oh, just a little place called Monks Corner. No monks anymore, though, and the corner isn't much to remark on, either." His mouth turned up in a sly smile, and James rolled his eyes theatrically at the man's witticism.

"My family owns a tobacco plantation in Virginia, on the Summerton Creek."

Oaker looked thoughtful. "Never heard of it, any more than you'd heard of Monks Corner before this very day, but that's no impediment."

He peered out toward the road that led out of town. "I suppose that you know that we're to march for Charles-Town."

It wasn't a question, but James answered anyway. "Aye. I'd guess that the enemy plans to do likewise to that city as they've done here."

Paul scowled. "I surely hope that it does not come to that," he said. "The trade has been interrupted badly enough with the ports being threatened. Should they come wholly under the control of the British, well, the war might as well be over in the parts I know."

James frowned. "Is it truly so bad as that?"

"It could be even worse than I make it out to be. Charles-

Town is where nearly all of the cargo from all across the southern colonies passes through. My grandfather tells stories from his childhood of the terrible disruptions when the infamous pirate Blackbeard blocked up the shipping for just a week, and I shudder to think of how much more we depend upon that port in the modern era."

James kept his reaction off of his face, but he felt instant skepticism at the mention of piracy, never mind a foe with as ridiculous a name as "Blackbeard."

He had heard his father scoff at tales of piracy on the high seas and in the Caribbean, dismissing them as the excuses of merchants who didn't want to confess that they'd dumped cargo when the weather looked to be turning bad, and so it was hard for James to take seriously any claim that a pirate had upset the trade for the whole of the south.

Paul was continuing, though, and James returned his attention to his new friend.

"I wasn't there, of course, but we repelled a British attempt at the city once before, so I should not expect that we will fail to do so a second time."

He grimaced. "In fact, one of the most notable men in that fight came to grief here at Savannah. Sergeant Jasper, who heroically raised our flag back up when it was shot down over Fort Moultrie, was here trying to achieve a similar feat. He had topped the wall over there at Spring Hill, and was raising our flag when those British scoundrels sent him to his reward with the colors still held tight in his hand."

James didn't have to exaggerate his gasp. "Why, I have heard of your Sergeant Jasper, but I had no idea that he was in our company, never mind that he had fallen here."

"Aye, 'tis just another awful loss we've suffered in this wretched place."

A shout from the next wagon up interrupted what would no doubt have been another lament for the cost and outcome of this campaign, and James was secretly glad for the intrusion.

"Oh, hey, that's the call to form up our wagons, and here I've been gossiping the morning away with you, instead of attending to my duties."

He looked over the contents of the wagon and grinned. "I suppose that it's good enough. If you don't mind, could you pass me the ropes from the other side, to secure the load before we move out?"

James moved to the other side of the wagon and busied himself with the light work, being mindful of the still-tender healing wound on his side. In short order, all was lashed tightly, making a padded platform onto which the soldiers' chests could now be arranged.

Waving a farewell to Paul, James returned to the former site of his company's encampment and got help from another man to bring own his chest over to the wagon. They hoisted the modest wooden box marked with James' name and containing all of his worldly possessions up onto the wagon and turned back to fetch the next.

Paul was engaged in a heated argument with a corporal who was insisting that his chest needed to be loaded at the back of the wagon for ease of access, regardless of how badly that might inconvenience other men.

As James was just far enough away that he could no longer hear the words being exchanged, he saw Paul clamber up onto the wagon and settle the matter by placing his boot on the side of the offending wooden chest and shoving it bodily off the back of the wagon. The chest sprang open, spilling its contents across the churned-up mud of the road, and James chuckled at the corporal's roar of indignation.

James shook his head at his new friend's lack of tact or proper respect for the privileges that ordinarily accompanied rank, but he suspected that the drover would not have taken a chance by resorting to such measures without being relatively sure that someone higher up would support his position, if not his methods.

When James returned, helping his messmate carry his chest, Paul was still fulminating, saying to another soldier, "No corporal will push me around, not when it comes to the balance of the load, or inconveniencing every other private soldier of the company for his own self interest. Why, I'll take it right up to the colonel, damme if I don't, and when I tell him that Corporal Dunford was putting the whole load in danger of tipping out on the road..."

Paul trailed off and directed James and his fellow soldier to place the chest they carried snugly against the one in front of it on the wagon. "We'll have just enough room for them all, I think, if the horses hold up," he remarked, and turned back to the soldier he'd been complaining to.

James' new sergeant came up from behind them, looking harried, and called out as he passed, "Make ready to form up, men. The colonel wants us on the road before noon, lest those pox-ridden British commanders take it into their heads to counterattack. Gather your gear, and be ready to march."

James sighed, and he and the other men hurried back to their former encampment to sling their gear for travel.

Chapter 15

James' feet hurt so much that he'd almost forgotten about the infernal itching around the healing wound in his side. The puckered pattern of holes where Doctor Perrault's needle had penetrated his flesh to sew up the furrow left by the passage of the British ball seemed to be the worst of it. It was all he could do to keep his hand off the fresh scar as he marched.

His company was far enough back in the column that the road was well and truly churned up by the time they passed over it, and James could make out Paul's shouts and curses from time to time over the incessant tromp and splash of soldier's boots, as his wagon struggled over the muck and ruts.

As Paul had feared, his horses were already weary. They had slowed to the point that the commander of the regiment himself had ridden back to learn what was holding up the company.

James was happy enough at the reduced pace, though. His wind was not as good as it had been before his injury, and their slow progress through the Carolina countryside gave him time to catch his breath.

The colonel was not satisfied, however, and once Paul explained to the commander that his horses were worn out, the officer rode off, returning shortly with a soldier leading a new team, doubtless "borrowed" from some other regiment.

The column ground to a halt long enough for Paul to switch

out the teams, and then they resumed their march, at a pace that had James panting.

However, as always, the rhythmic footfalls of the troops marching in step helped carry him along, and despite it being a faster pace than he might have wanted to set on his own, he was able enough to keep up.

The end of the day was very welcome, nonetheless, and once the troops had stopped, James gratefully threw off his pack. He could barely summon the energy to set out his bedroll before he laid down on the ground to nap.

He knew he had a short time before supper, while the men from his mess whose turn it was to cook that evening boiled up whatever they had left in their supplies.

As he drifted off he smelled the familiar odor of pease porridge, and stifled a groan. It might be filling, but the porridge left his gut feeling unsettled for hours after eating. Peas had never been his favorite food, but he had long since promised himself that if he survived the war, he would never again willingly eat them.

A rough kick at the bottom of his boot woke him from a fitful sleep, and he grunted his way into a sitting position.

"Supper's getting cold," the soldier who'd woken him said, and moved on to the next sleeping form. James didn't resent the gruff wake-up call — he expected that he, too, would be a bit on the irritable side at the sight of men snoring while he labored over a hot kettle.

He rose and accepted his portion, returning to sit on his bedroll as he ate, his back relaxed against the pack he'd been using as a pillow. He took a bite of the porridge and suppressed a grimace at the bland, unpleasant meal. It would have been far better with a rasher of bacon in it, or better yet, a smoked pork knuckle, but such luxuries were unheard of in the army of the United States.

The sergeant came around, and James nodded in greeting. The sergeant returned the acknowledgment and said, "Hatch, you're on guard duty until midnight. Eat up, then go relieve the man on this side of the road, so he can have his supper while it's still warm."

James kept his feelings on this development out of his tone. "Aye, sir." The sergeant nodded again, and moved on, leaving James with his thoughts.

In fairness, this was the first time since they'd departed from Savannah that he'd pulled guard duty, but still, he wasn't looking forward to having to walk around just to try to keep from freezing in the night chill.

He did not want to cost the man he would relieve the opportunity to relish the "*delicious*" supper, though, so he hurried through shoveling the mushy green porridge into his mouth, and stood, his feet lodging a fresh protest as he put his weight on them again.

At least his side had quit itching — until he had that thought, whereupon it immediately began itching more than it had all day. He sighed and controlled the urge to scratch, gathering up his musket and gear, and then leaving to seek out the guard whose place he was to take.

As he made his way through the field full of bedrolls thrown down as haphazardly as his own had been, the setting sun cast a baleful, sickly orange glow over everything, and the appearance it gave to the irregularly-clumped men sitting or lying down against their packs put James in mind of nothing so much as a leaf of tobacco overrun by beetles. He caught himself questioning whether God himself saw them that same way, as pests to be swept away, but he shook himself and dismissed the bitter thought.

At the edge of the impromptu camp, the guard on duty stood staring out at the sun on the horizon, lost in thought. When he turned around, James saw that it was Patrick, and he permitted himself to wonder for a moment why good men like Thomas and Henri could be blotted out of existence, while a man of such narrow understanding as Patrick could thrive.

Brusquely, he said, "I'm to relieve you, so that you may sup."

Patrick frowned, but said nothing as he took his leave.

James stared at the man as he walked away, puzzled as to how he could see with his own eyes the evidence of the humanity of the men of the *Chasseurs-Volontaires*, and still cling to the belief that they were no more than animals, only because their skin was a different color than his own.

James turned away from the camp and looked out over the field where they had set up for the night. Some farmer was going to come out in the morning and survey the leavings of this army. Would he be happy that his land had provided a resting place, or resentful of the disruption their passage represented?

At least they were traveling outside of the growing season, so they weren't damaging any crops.

Still, James knew there were plenty of men in these districts who felt loyalty to the King, and wished the rebels nothing but ill. He thought idly about whether the generals had bothered to ask the landowners if they objected to their fields being used to bed down the regiments for a night, or just trusted that the sheer number of men under arms would quiet any opposition that might exist in the hearts of the farmers.

The sun slipped down below the horizon entirely, its last light fading as James moved slowly along the perimeter of the encampment, his thoughts darting from one thing to the next, without any particular direction.

How odd it had been that Claude had clutched the last remains of their friend Henri. The unknown, but likely tragic fate of Prevard, who had survived so much in his life. The suggestion that Doctor Perrault had made that James might be cut out to pursue the avocation of medicine.

That last made him snort to himself as he considered what his father's reaction would be. Doubtless, the older man would find it uproariously funny that his son would be thought to have the prodigious mental capacity required to undertake the study of medicine. In truth, humors and bone-setting, bloodletting, and amputation, and everything else that a doctor was called upon to do seemed terribly complex to James, and he scoffed at the idea of exploring the thought further.

He pondered Patrick's behavior again. The man seemed almost offended that the Negro soldiers had fought as gallantly as anyone else, as though he would have been more comforted in his beliefs to have seen them behave like the lesser creatures he claimed them to be.

In light of the fact that a detachment of these volunteers had been assigned to the relatively undistinguished duty of attending to the sick and hurt, it would seem that Patrick was not alone in underestimating their capacities.

Somewhere in the tree line at the distant edge of the field,

James heard a creature — perhaps a mouse of some sort — squeak in protest at being taken by a predator, and shuddered slightly when the cries abruptly cut off.

Just because it was the way of the world didn't mean he had to like it.

With the sun below the horizon, the evening chill descended quickly. James walked briskly along the edge of the encampment, until he could see the guard responsible for the next segment staring toward him. He gave that man a wave of acknowledgment and turned back the other way.

He soon saw the guard for the segment at the other end of his own area of responsibility, and turned back again.

Walking steadily back and forth between sightings of his fellow guards, James fell into a routine, counting his paces so that as the light failed further, he would still cover the length of his portion of the picket.

At some point, he stopped abruptly, realizing he had fallen asleep on his feet. Peering around him to see what had interrupted his walking doze, he thought he saw a dark form out in the field, which was lit now by the waxing moon.

He challenged, "Who goes there?"

The form froze, and then came back his direction.

Out of the half-darkness, James heard a voice call out, "*Memoire, et revenge, et fraternité, mon ami.*" Claude's face appeared then in the moonlight, his hands up in surrender.

Chapter 16

J ames stared at the Frenchman's open, raised hands for a long moment, before blurting out, "What on earth are you doing, Claude?"

The man had his full traveling pack on his back and his musket slung, as though he were setting out on a day's march instead of recovering from one.

Although the French soldier couldn't understand his words, he seemed to grasp what James was asking, for he answered in French, shaking his head slowly and dropping his chin to his chest.

James thought he heard Henri's name in the long explanation that Claude offered, but he couldn't be certain.

In that moment, he wished that he had been able to learn more French than just the few words that might be barked out to coordinate the loading and firing sequence for a line of muskets. Sighing deeply, he motioned for Claude to follow him, so that he could seek out his sergeant and ask the man for guidance as to what to do.

He suspected that Claude had been in the process of deserting — a shocking number of both French and American forces had disappeared into the darkness during the nights following their defeat at Savannah, though the penalties for doing so could be severe. But what he could not make sense of was why the French soldier had been so close to the American regiments, if that were the case.

The way to the woods at the edge of the field was relatively visible, particularly in the moonlight, yet Claude had come up this way instead. As he walked back into the encampment, Claude trailed behind him, his bearing giving an impression of determination, rather than shame or fear.

James found his sergeant's bedroll, and crouched beside the man, speaking in a quiet, urgent tone, "Sir, I need your advice."

The sergeant awoke at once, his eyes wide and his hands already questing for the musket by his side. He paused and squinted into the darkness, recognizing James and looking past him at Claude.

"Caught yourself a blackbird, did you?"

"Nay, sir, not exactly. This is Corporal Legrand from one of the French regiments, with whom I served at Savannah. He was a part of the detail that was assigned to help us establish ourselves there, and later, I was sent to duty alongside his squad, guarding the entrenchments as those were being established." He paused, unsure what to add to that introduction.

The sergeant nodded and said, "Go on. What is the corporal doing away from the sick and hurt encampment, and among our men?"

"Well, that's the thing . . . he speaks no English, and I no French. We've always communicated through another French soldier, but that man was apparently lost in the attack on Spring Hill."

"I see. So we need a translator."

"Aye, sir."

The sergeant sighed and clambered to his feet. "Very well.

I believe there are some men among the wounded who can help us. Come with me, and bring your friend."

The term was used without malice, but James couldn't help but feel a chill at the possibility that Claude's attempt to leave his service behind could come back to reflect on him somehow.

James fell into step behind the sergeant, and together with Claude, they made their way through the slumbering men up to the road. Although the moon was dropping in the sky, there was still enough light to move by, and they made good time back to the section of the column where the wounded and the *Chasseurs-Volontaires* who'd been assigned to care for them were set up.

At the roadside, they were challenged in French by a guard, and the sergeant growled back, "We're Americans. Take us to someone who speaks English."

James could see the guard's brow furrow, but after a brief hesitation, the man slung his musket back over his shoulder and pointed toward the far end of the field, then led them in that direction.

There, he spoke in rapid-fire French to another guard, who answered him sleepily, and then turned to face the sergeant. In heavily-accented, halting English, he said, "You are needing for translation?"

"Yes," the sergeant said. He began to add more, but the French soldier interrupted him.

"Who speaks the French?" The sergeant pointed beyond James, to where Claude stood, waiting. The French soldier's eyebrows went up a tiny bit, but he addressed Claude in French, his tone still sleepy and calm.

Claude replied, and the two conversed for a while, and

James got the impression from the guard's tone and hand motions that he was having a hard time understanding what Claude was telling him, even in his own language.

Eventually, the guard turned back to the sergeant. "This one, he says he has an obligation for to return and avenge the deaths of his brothers at Savannah. He also says that he came for to seek for that man" — he gestured toward James — "because of he thought that he, too might have an obligation in this matter."

The guard threw his hands up in evident frustration. "I have explained to him, that we in this army do not observe personal obligations for revenge, but are required to obey the orders we given. If it should happen that this permits us an opportunity for revenge, well, so much the better. But to go away on a personal mission, this is not permitted."

Claude was scowling now, his chin jutting out defiantly.

The sergeant turned to James now, his expression quizzical. "Private, do you know anything of this mission of revenge?"

James swallowed hard and tried to explain. "After the cannon ambush at the trench, several of us got together and swore an oath to one another, promising to remember the dead, and to avenge them, but I have not since discussed this with any of those who were present. Corporal Legrand and I are, I believe, the last of that group still alive, so I must presume he believed that I would join him in fulfilling this rum oath."

The French guard's eyebrows shot up now. "A rum oath, you say? That is a very serious matter, as such oaths are not permitted in our service."

He turned back to Claude, questioning him in a tone that was suddenly more serious, and James felt a chill rush over him. It had not been his intention to cause trouble for his friend, but only to explain what might have been driving the man's actions.

After another few minutes of back-and-forth in French, the guard faced James again. "The corporal tells me that he was not aware of the prohibition against the rum oath. I have told him that under the regulations of this army, he is released from any obligation of such an oath, and he has accepted that. He has also agreed that he will not attempt his mission again, but will wait for the opportunity to seek revenge when it is possible within the boundaries of his orders."

The guard looked James in the eye. "You must also agree to this, so that Corporal Legrand may know that you will not pursue for vengeance without him."

James nodded quickly, and Claude caught his eye, his head shaking in a barely perceptible dismissal.

Did Claude mean that he was rejecting the conditions this man was imposing, or was he disappointed that James was not abiding by the oath they had taken with Prevard?

He could not tell, but James' heart dropped at the thought that Claude might believe he was so easily abandoning the promise he'd made. However, aloud, he said, "If Clau- I mean. Corporal Legrand is satisfied to leave the fulfillment of his promise to avenge our friend's death at the time and place of the army's choosing, then I am likewise satisfied."

The sergeant shot James an inscrutable look, but said nothing.

The French soldier nodded briskly, "I will see this man back to his place in the camp, and remind our guards that we are to be looking for not only enemies approaching, but also for friends who are attempting to depart."

The sergeant dipped his head in acknowledgment, and gathered James up with a gesture. "I will get my man back to his duty on the picket, and remind our guards of the same." James glanced back at Claude as he left, and found the man's eyes on him, steadfast and serious. He nodded his farewell, and Claude nodded back, without expression.

As they walked back toward their own company's section of the encampment, the other man asked James, conversationally, "How did you come to be so enmeshed with these French Negroes?"

He considered for a long moment how best to answer the question, and finally settled on simply, "They were good soldiers. I saw that they were no less gallant, no less brave, no less dedicated than any of their fellows — and in many cases, were more so. They are devoted to one another, and they are good men."

The sergeant said nothing for several paces. "And this rum oath, what on earth is that?"

James explained Thomas' death, and the gathering to memorialize the lost man, concluding, "What could be wrong with swearing to remember and avenge a man who was as a brother to us? Would we do any less for a member of our own company, when he had given his last breath to the cause of our independence?"

"No, I suppose not, so it surprises me somewhat that the French officers should have disapproved of the practice."

James thought about that, and then said, "It may be that the sentiment is fine, but they do not want gunpowder being used in the ceremony, when it ought to be driving musket and cannon shot toward the enemy."

The man stopped in the road and stared at James, his eyes

wide in astonishment. "You drank *powder?*"

James grinned sheepishly, though the moonlight did not provide enough illumination for the other man to see his expression. "In honesty, I did not know that there was powder in the rum until after I drank it. I just thought it was an uncommonly strong bottle, and that we were toasting Private Lambert's memory."

With a thoughtful tone, he continued, "Regardless, I am proud to have been invited to join in their oath, and will be glad to be able to deliver on it when we face the enemy again."

"It sounded as though Corporal Legrand intended to find the exact men who killed his friend, and do to them what he thought the oath demanded of him. I don't doubt that he could have done it, too . . . posed as a deserter, gained their trust, and sought out his targets."

The sergeant nodded, and James could almost imagine that his tone was approving as he started up the road again.

"We would all do well to have such friends in this conflict. I only hope that it augurs well for the devotion of the rest of the French force to our cause."

"I hope so, too, sir."

James could just make out the man's frown. "I have a name, Hatch. Sergeant James Borland, originally from Charles-Town. Your former sergeant, Edward Barker, spoke well of you . . . although he did mention that you had some sort of fight with one of the men in the company, and that he was endeavoring to keep you apart."

James ducked his head in embarrassment at the revelation that his conduct *had* attracted the attention he had hoped to avoid. He said, reluctantly, "Aye, Sergeant Borland, although it has been some time now since that incident."

Sergeant Borland grunted in acknowledgment, and said, "Sergeant Barker never named the other man, nor did he commit anything to his official reports or the private journal I found among his effects. If you should like for me to continue to keep you apart from this man, say his name, and I'll do my best."

James answered hurriedly, "Nay, sir, let us forget about it entirely. It was a private matter, and I think it may have been solved now."

The sergeant glanced over at him, and said, "Just remember that we cannot tolerate fights over dice or other games. No debt incurred over the bones is sufficient cause to undermine our company's ability to take the fight to our real enemy."

James answered, "Aye, sir, I understand."

Inwardly, he was relieved that the sergeant suspected his fight with Patrick had been over a dice game, and not over a question of philosophy. A debt could be settled, with no lasting hard feelings, but it was harder to reconcile seeing the *Chasseurs-Volontaires* as human beings rather than nothing more than animals.

Stopping as they neared the sleeping forms of the men of their company, Borland whispered to James, "Return to your post on the picket, and keep a sharp eye out, as the French guard reminded us. It was good to get to know you a bit better, Hatch."

He clapped James on the shoulder and sent him on his way to gaze into the darkness as the moon set completely behind the tree line.

When his relief arrived after endless hours of counting his steps in the darkness, James returned to his own bedroll, but despite being weary from a day of marching and late night duty, he had a hard time settling his mind enough to get to sleep.

He wondered if he had done the right thing by bringing Claude back to his detail, and whether he had fulfilled the oath he'd taken with his friend, or violated it.

Thinking about Claude's defiant head shake, he decided that the French soldier had no intention of considering himself released from the oath, which told him, too, that the other man would consider James to still be bound by it as well.

In his heart, James did want revenge against the British for what they had done to his friends . . . never mind what they'd done in taking and holding the unfortunate town of Savannah.

Chapter 17

After spending so many nights sleeping in the open air, with only the thin bedroll between his back and whatever roots or rocks had escaped his notice, having an actual tent over him again was strange for James.

The comfort, such as it was, came at a price.

"Having held Savannah against our most strenuous efforts, there is little doubt that the British commanders will now set their sights once again on this fair city," their lieutenant said, after the column of weary soldiers had come to a halt before the tumbled-down fortifications of Charles-Town.

He motioned to the crumbling embankment, which was already being overtaken with grass, vines, and other weeds. "When they arrive, they must find these walls impregnable."

The officer turned and pointed out to the bay before the city. "You have all heard, I am sure, about the enemy's failure to take Fort Moultrie, out beyond the harbor. We repelled them that time, and we will repel them again, but we must act in haste to be ready for their attack."

James and the men around him stirred uncomfortably at the thought of doing anything in haste other than getting some well-deserved rest, but the lieutenant continued.

"Once we have recovered ourselves from our journey hence, the general has assigned this company to build up walls to the rear portion of the fortification they call the Horn Work, so as to provide our forces with a place of retreat that can accommodate the entire army, should the need arise."

Before dismissing them, the lieutenant concluded by instructing the company to set up their encampment in good order, and in anticipation of long occupation of this place.

The soldier to James' right had stage-whispered, "We *hope* it will be a long occupation, but the enemy may have other ideas." James had shot the man a sardonic grin.

While setting up his tent, James looked up at the odd, rough surface of the wall that the lieutenant had indicated. Sergeant Borland came by and saw him gazing at it.

"They built that some twenty years past, out of stuff they called 'tappy,' to defend the city should the French come calling."

James snorted and looked pointedly toward where the *Chasseurs-Volontaires* were setting up their own tents, their colors snapping in the breeze. "Time turns everything around and sets it on its face, doesn't it?"

"Aye, it does at that. 'Tis passing strange that fate should now bring the French to help us hold the city at these same walls from the British who ordered them to be built." He shrugged. "Wouldn't be the first time that such a thing happened, though, and I dare say that it won't be the last."

James eyed the wall with curiosity again. "What is 'tappy?' I've never heard of that kind of stone before."

"Oh, it's not a natural stone at all, but rather a sort of concrete, made by burning up oyster shells to free the lime in them, then mixing that with sand, and rocks, and more shells, in just enough water so that it flows. We then pour that into forms that have been constructed beforehand, and wait for it to dry up."

He shrugged. "Before the war, I used it to help build a couple of walls and a root cellar, as the stuff is easier to work with than brick — and faster, to boot." He gestured up at the Horn Work. "Those walls haven't been tried by cannon yet, but I have a feeling they'll hold up all right."

James nodded. "That wall looks like a single piece of rock, carved to the purpose. *I* should not like to be asked to attack it."

The sergeant barked a laugh. "It does look even more imposing than the earthen walls we faced at Savannah. Let us hope that the enemy finds them as impossible to overcome."

James dipped his head, "I shall indeed hope for that, though I will hope more fervently that the British generals decide some other target is more worthy of their attention. I have no desire to serve on both sides of a siege, sir."

Borland grinned merrily. "None of us do. Indeed, 'tis the fondest wish of very soldier to serve his time in a comfortable tent, and never be exposed to the enemy's threats. You may have noticed that we have not been so blessed by fortune thus far."

James nodded in reluctant agreement, and waved farewell to the sergeant. "Thank you for the cheerful thought, sir. I'll remember you in my prayers, alongside the prayer that you shall be proved wrong." Borland laughed and walked away, leaving James to resume unrolling his tent.

Now, as the night sounds surrounded him, James wondered what the other side of a siege *would* be like. He had heard talk about the privation the British must have suffered in being unable to resupply from either the countryside around Savannah or the river, which was hemmed in by the French, and wondered whether the British would be able to so easily blockade this port.

In addition, Savannah had been surrounded by very difficult country, with swamps and marshes standing in the way of all but a few approaches, and those, the French and American forces had been able to sever. What he'd seen of the countryside coming into Charles-Town, though, there were many ways through, and cutting off its communication with the outside world would require an enormous force of men.

He shook his head and turned over on his bedroll, willing himself to let these thoughts leave his mind. He was no military strategist — all he could do was rehash the things he'd heard others comment on. But somehow, he felt more comfortable about their position in this city than he would have on the other side of the line in Savannah.

When the morning came, he was far too busy with the heavy work demanded of his company to give the matter further thought. He had been assigned to extend the long, deep trench that stood before the completed portion of the Horn Work, loading the heavy, wet clay he dug up onto carts. Those were hauled to the top, where they were added to the height of the new breastwork extending the tappy wall southward.

The digging was difficult, repetitive work, and James' scar, which hadn't bothered him in several days, was burning and itching before the sun had made its way fully over the top of the fortifications. He deliberately set his mind to cataloging his other aches, if only to distract himself from wanting to scratch and tear at the line of angry pink flesh on his side.

Sergeant Borland came around at midday, and James asked him, perhaps in a more irritable tone than intended, "Why are we not simply building forms to build the wall of tappy, as you described to me yesterday?"

Borland smiled indulgently. "The stuff takes far too long to prepare and cure out. The enemy could be here before we finish three courses of it, and to match the height of this portion of the Horn Work would require perhaps ten or more. And each must dry completely before another is added atop it, else it will all just burst out of the forms and flow out like a river."

James scowled. "Then the British should have finished this job, back when they were preparing a welcome for the French. Must we perpetually be finishing what they have started?"

Sergeant Borland laughed out loud. "Do you not perceive that that is exactly what we are engaged in doing, on the broadest scale? They may have started this country, but they have neglected and misused it. As a consequence, we are left to wrest it from their hands and finish building upon the stalwart beginnings they have given us."

He grinned. "There's a cheering thought for you as you dig, private. We may be finishing what they started, but in the end, it will be all ours to enjoy."

James frowned, but kept his opinions to himself. He felt certain that by the end of a day of this work, he would be just as happy to let them keep the whole blasted thing.

Sleep that night was easier than it had been even when they were marching, and a fortnight of hard labor ensured that James had little energy left to ponder the broader questions of their purpose in this work, or his role in it.

All he had the capacity to do was to push his spade into the soil, cut out another block of clay, and heave it onto the cart, over and over again.

The men to either side of him were no more able to carry on a conversation, and James passed the days in a dull sort of stupor.

After a week or so of this brute labor, an officer from the French engineer corps came around and looked over the trench they had cut, and the earthworks resulting above. He nodded approvingly and addressed the work crew, looking up at the far end of the trench from where they stood.

His accent made him sound vaguely aristocratic as he said, "I believe this is enough here, and we can turn to filling this trench with the water, so as to provide a more substantial barrier to the enemy."

James heard groans from around him, and his own thoughts echoed them. For the last few days, they had been digging with water rising up to their ankles and higher. The thought of having to make that problem even more pronounced sounded deeply unpleasant.

The engineering officer seemed surprised at their response, and turned to look at the men. "Oh, do not worry, you will not be obliged to labor in the ditch after it is filled. We need only to build a little dam down at that end, and the water that has been flowing through here will be collected to confound the British, not you."

James had his doubts about what might constitute a "little dam," but he suppressed them. The prospect of being able to again work with his feet dry was enough to cheer him up a bit.

The engineering corps officer squinted at the breastwork rising above them and pointed at its face. "If you men can but cut that so it lies a bit closer to the vertical, rather than leaving it as an easy ramp for the enemy to climb, I will declare myself satisfied with it." He then gestured to the top of the embankment. "I will have the crew at the top shift from using a cart to bring up the fill from here, to using buckets on a winch, so that we can leave no path for an attack, should the enemy get this far."

Having casually delivered this pronouncement, the man reached down and flicked a spot of mud from his boot.

James had never known that such an innocuous-seeming act could fill him with such rage. His own shoes were waterlogged and ruined, and this man could not tolerate a single spot of mud? If he had been closer, James might have been tempted to arrange for some mishap that would coat the officer in muck from toe to crown.

The officer waved cheerily and turned to climb back out of the trench, oblivious to the seething soldiers he left behind.

Once he was out of earshot, one man asked the group, "Have you ever seen such a dandy?"

James was inclined to agree with the sentiment, though he didn't say anything.

Another soldier growled, "He'd have looked just as much at home had he been wielding a whip and calling us blackbirds."

"Oh, come now," a third man mock-scolded. "Everyone knows that a slave has more rights than does a soldier, when there's earthworks to be raised!"

There was general laughter, although James didn't join in. The undertone of the comment struck him as being ugly and dangerous.

A man who was enslaved, he knew, could be assaulted or even killed by his master for any reason — or no reason at all — and nobody would think less of his assailant, save perhaps for the waste of capital. However, a soldier was safe from such mistreatment, and to pretend otherwise was to feign ignorance of the plight of the slave.

James kept his reaction off of his face. There was no sense in stirring up trouble over a casual jest, so he simply clambered up out of the water, making his way to the face of the embankment that the officer had directed be reshaped.

The other men followed him, still grumbling among themselves, and they all set to examining how they ought to approach the new task.

In the end, there was nothing they could do until the winches were set up above, so James glanced around, saw that no sergeant or other officer was within sight, and found a comfortable place on the slope to catch some rest.

Chapter 18

The official took off his glasses and made a long production out of wiping them clean with a handkerchief, before setting them carefully down on the table.

"So, you served at Savannah, and then proceeded to the defense of Charleston?"

"Aye, it's as I've said, isn't it?"

The other man put his glasses back on, hooking first one ear loop on and then the other. "Very well, then. You told me earlier that this Legrand fellow was remarkably brave, yet you've had little to say about him after his friend — another of the soldiers from Saint-Domingue, that is to say, Haiti, I presume? — was killed at Savannah."

"Oh, yes, I haven't yet gotten to that part, as it happened later, at Charles-Town. Not that he wasn't brave at Savannah, but at Charles-Town, he distinguished himself to an even more remarkable degree..."

⚬◯⚬

"The general is most pleased with your efforts to fortify this town, particularly given the extreme lack of support and supplies from the people of this state." The captain scowled, but he did not give voice to the source of his irritation beyond what he'd already said.

"We have endeavored to send for laborers from the country

around this town, but the laws of the state of South-Carolina do not permit the general to lay an absolute command that they be provided. As you know, this has obliged him to ask *you* to labor as though you were indentured instead of enlisted, and the general has asked me to convey to you his humblest apologies for that necessity."

The man behind James snorted so hard that he could feel the soldier's breath on the back on his neck. James remained stock still, though, lest the captain's sharp glance in his direction mistake him for the culprit of this expression of derision.

The company had, in fact, been performing common labor since the moment of their arrival at Charles-Town. It had initially been passed off as a temporary measure, until proper resources could be secured — which, James had come to understand, meant slaves, pressed into the service of the army over the objections of their masters.

When one piece of heavy work after another had been completed without relief from that quarter, there had been talk of at least making the soldiers from Saint-Domingue take up labor, and finding some other means of caring for those wounded and sick who still needed help.

James had learned of this when Claude had appeared at James' tent one evening, his face shining with happy excitement. He'd brought along another man to translate for him, who quickly introduced himself in clear, barely-accented English as Marc. The two French soldiers sat on their heels to talk with James, who was just finishing up his supper.

Claude could hardly slow down enough to permit the other soldier to relate what he was saying, so it took a while for James to get a clear understanding of what had Claude so excited.

Rumor was, Claude explained through Marc, that there had been a shouting match between two colonels of the American forces. One of them was demanding that the *Chasseurs-Volontaires* be treated as ordinary Negroes, driven before the whip as slaves. The other declared that the soldiers from Saint-Domingue deserved to be granted all of the protections and privileges of any other unit of militia.

The argument had been brought before the general, who had forcefully come down on the side of treating the French force as soldiers.

Claude grinned and said something in an affected deep voice, and his translator relayed, "The general say, 'If we turn those men slaves, in reward for their brave fight at Savannah, we will never again be able ask for help from any black man in the whole country. They will turn against us and fight for the British instead.'"

James nodded thoughtfully. Such a betrayal of the *Chasseurs-Volontaires* would have not only soured the rest of their regiment on supporting the American cause, but could even have undermined the alliance with the French in general.

He replied, "I am happy to hear that we have some men of good sense among the officers here."

Marc relayed the message, and then listened to Claude's response, and his own chin bobbed in agreement as he said, "We like that your general does not let us be turned to slaves, that he understand that we have fought and deserve be treated as men, and not animals."

He added, "Claude say general reminds him of you."

James was flattered to be compared to the commander

of the army at Charles-Town; even better, Claude felt that the commander measured up to to a standard that *James* had set, whether he'd meant to or not.

He dipped his head in acknowledgment of the compliment. "Certainly, I am not the only member of this army who can see what is obvious. You are men, like any other in this world, and you do not need to demonstrate any extraordinary bravery or feats of strength for a person of good conscience to take note of that plain fact."

He frowned, and confessed, "I regret that it did take witnessing such things for *me* to understand this, but I am a simple soldier from a Virginia farm, and do not have the sophistication of an officer in this army."

He did not add that he had dark suspicions that, like Patrick, many of those officers were so wedded to their view of the world that they would refuse to acknowledge such self-evident truths, regardless of what feats and deeds they witnessed.

Marc translated for Claude, and the two of them conversed for a while before Marc told James, "Claude says that he saw the care you gave to Thomas when he fell." He glanced over to the other French soldier, and added, in a more somber tone, "And he experienced your care for himself, when he lost his dear Henri."

Claude's chin fell to his chest at the mention of Henri's name, and James bowed his head in respect for Claude's grief. Marc continued, "Claude told me of the rum oath, and said that with Corporal Prevard lost in the action at Savannah, only you and he remain to fulfill that oath."

James looked up sharply at Marc. "Corporal Prevard was indeed lost, then?"

Marc said, "Yes, that is what Claude has told me. He never returned to his company, and must have been among those who were buried at Savannah."

James pressed his lips together tightly to try to forestall his tears. He nodded his acknowledgment of the obligation, unmet and — he now knew — proscribed under the rules of the French army. The tally of revenge owed seemed to grow ever longer.

Marc gave him an approving glance. "A simple man would not have sworn such an oath with soldiers who he did not believe to be fellow men. You give yourself too little respect. And there is no shame in having risen above your prior understanding of the world."

He waved a dismissive hand. "I, for one, am glad to have made your acquaintance, and I hope that you can soon repay the oath that you have sworn against the British."

He rose, and Claude stood up beside him. The tall French soldier caught James' eye, and intoned, "*Memoire, et revenge, et fraternité.*"

James stood as well, and clasped Claude's hands between both of his own, and repeated, "Memory, and revenge, and brotherhood, my friend."

The Frenchmen left to return to their part of the encampment, and James was left to ponder the meaning of the rumor they'd related, and how it might play out in the days to come.

Happily, there had been no hint of a change in the general's sentiment, and the *Chasseurs-Volontaires* had continued their difficult and demanding role as caretakers to the wounded and sick — which the regiments working to build up the defenses of

Charles-Town seemed to add to on a daily basis. A man cutting wood might slip and take off a toe with his axe, or the foul air around the walls of the old fort would sicken an entire detail.

There was nothing new about men getting hurt or falling ill in the conduct of their duties as soldiers, but the frequency with which it happened under the difficult conditions here meant that there was no slackening of the demand for the services of the French detachment to care for them.

James realized that his mind had wandered, and he was yanked out of his reflections on the treatment of the French soldiers as the captain spoke again.

"Having gotten a satisfactory wall completed here at the southern extent of the Horn Work, and a dam raised to fill the ditch before it, the general has asked that two battalions be sent out to Sullivan's Island, offshore from the city proper, to restore Fort Moultrie to something like wartime readiness, and stand ready to defend the harbor, should the enemy again think to approach by sea."

The company stood stock still, but James could feel his fellow soldiers restraining their dismay. There would be no relief from the heavy work of the past months.

The captain continued, "You may have heard stories of the soft wood of the walls that so surprised and confounded the British assault when it caught and held their cannon balls, instead of splintering into projectiles that would, themselves, impale and maim men."

He grimaced. "It has been nearly four years since that time, and while the wood was advantageous then, its condition has declined rapidly, and will now scarcely hold back the earthworks.

Worse, there are no ditches before the walls, nor pickets, nor abatis, and I do not have to remind you how effective all of those are at discouraging an attempt to force entry into a stronghold."

More than one man frowned sourly at the statement, but the captain continued without acknowledging their reactions.

"We will be moving our encampment out to the fortification there on Sullivan's Island. Until the state sees fit to supply us with the laborers we require, we will endeavor to remedy these shortcomings ourselves . . . while also maintaining ourselves and our equipment in a state of preparedness against the possibility of an attack without warning."

A few men did groan aloud at this, and the captain offered a mollifying gesture with his hands. "We have no intelligence of such an effort in the offing, as the enemy seems to currently be intent on stirring up trouble for us among the residents of the back country around these parts, in order to discourage them from supporting the cause of independence."

Grimacing again, as though at some private discontent, the captain added, "It is no secret that a great proportion of the inhabitants of the back country in this state are at best indifferent to the cause, and at worst openly unfriendly to it."

He squared his shoulders and looked over the assembled ranks of men. "Nonetheless, we shall gain them their independence and defend them against the mistreatment of the British army and what allies it can gather. We do not require their open gratitude in order to make this effort on their behalf. Our duty to our nation is clear, and we will execute it despite the difficulties."

He indicated the open water beyond the city, and the island they were bound for. "There is little danger at the moment of an attempt from the sea, as the weather is hostile during this season to travel by water. So, once we have the fortifications on the island in good order, it will be a very defensible location. With the work that we have already done to improve upon our positions here at the approaches to the city, we should have little to fear of any enemy attempt on this place."

He clapped his hands, and one man to James' left jumped a little, as though awoken from a standing nap. "Let us prepare to move our encampment, then, and on the morrow, once we are established at Fort Moultrie, we will begin the work of ensuring that we may hold it against any threat."

He nodded to the lieutenant and took his leave of the company. The lieutenant in turn dismissed the men with an order to busy themselves with breaking down their encampment.

As they moved toward their tent, one of James' messmates remarked, "Captain says 'we' a whole lot for a man who won't be on the wrong end of a shovel."

James said nothing, but he was hard-pressed to disagree.

Chapter 19

The encampment inside the walls at Fort Moultrie was abuzz with rumors, fueled by the appearance in the harbor of six ships that were excitedly identified as captured British transports and warships.

Within an hour of the ships' arrival, under the watchful eyes of their American captors, word was spreading that they had been part of an enormous fleet of over one hundred — no, *two* hundred — British ships, come to invade and take South-Carolina by overwhelming force.

James listened to the stories being passed around him from man to man with a mixture of skepticism and growing dread. He was working beside Private Oaker, the man he'd met loading the supply train at the evacuation from Savannah, and they were, as were all around them, discussing the implications of the news.

Oaker said, "While we know from bitter personal experience that having the larger army does not guarantee victory, it will certainly mean a return to fighting, in place of labor."

James retorted, "Of the two, I prefer labor. I haven't been shot even once while wielding a shovel."

Oaker shrugged. "I am glad for the distraction from the digging, woodcutting, stake-pounding, and whatever else the engineering corps might devise for us to do, but it looks like the captain was wrong about the enemy's appetite for travel through the weather of the season."

James snorted and said, "More than that, though, it proves that the British have serious intent about taking these southern states. They must believe that by doing so, they can weaken the resolve of the Congress, or even remove from them the ability to resist any longer at all."

Oaker frowned. "There is something to that." He gestured at the fort around them. "If the general is right, though, we may be able to persuade the enemy to waste his efforts here, and break *their* capacity to continue the war any further."

James laughed, the sound harsh even in his own ears. "While I should like very much to see this be the rock upon which the British wave breaks and is dissipated, I would be happier to not stand between the rock and the wave when that happens."

Oaker joined in James' laughter, saying, "I am not made to be a barnacle in the surf, that is certain." He held out his arm and pinched the skin at his wrist. "For one thing, my skin is far too delicate to stand up to any kind of abuse of that nature."

James nodded, pulling up the side of his shirt to display the long, puckered scar where he had been shot. "I have already tested that question for myself, and I am satisfied that I should not like at all to try it a second time."

He shook his head, tucking his shirt back into his breeches. "No, let the wave break somewhere else, and let us here just be a quiet, unremarked stone on a distant hill, safe to observe it from afar."

"I think we should all like that," Oaker agreed. "But for today, if we do not finish digging out and placing the stakes along this portion of the wall, some damnable officer of the engineering corps will have a word with the lieutenant, who will send the sergeant here to make us wish we were facing the enemy instead."

James laughed again, and picked up his shovel, turning his back on the small convoy of captured British ships now being ushered into the inner harbor.

Over the next few days, enough information filtered out about the ships and men taken captive to almost make James feel sorry for them. However, the very presence of the expedition made it increasingly clear that the enemy had indeed sent a large force to attack the southern states.

One British ship, he heard from a soldier who had helped to unload the seized supplies found aboard it, had departed from New-York with 45 horses aboard — mounts for a company of dragoons also taken prisoner — but only two of the animals had survived the passage.

The man who'd been employed at what might otherwise have been a victorious job said with a sad shake of his head, "'Twas a sorry business, clearing out the equipment for the lost steeds. The two horses we did take were both in sorry shape, having been much tossed about by storms after their departure."

James said, "So it seems that the general supposition that the enemy would not have embarked upon an expedition to these parts due to the ocean weather of this season was not unfounded . . . but they are so eager to challenge us here that they decided to chance it anyway."

"Aye, and it cost them dear. Our little squadron only took these ships because they had got separated from their convoy in the weather, and were without the support of any heavier ships, or so the fellows on our frigates tell me."

James shuddered. "I have never been aboard a ship, and hearing these stories gives me no desire to change that. A storm on land is trouble enough, but at least the land doesn't answer the wind by leaping up and dashing you against the walls of your room."

The other man shrugged. "Each mode of travel and life is attended by its own collection of risks and rewards. I should like very much to see more of the world than just what lies within a day's journey by horse. Why, in a single day, a ship might travel as far as a man does on foot in a fortnight."

"If it gets there at all," James retorted. "Witness our inadvertent guests."

The other man smiled. "The same risks may be found on land during wartime. We hear all the time about patrols of our side or the other being taken prisoner, do we not?"

"Aye, that we do, yet we scarcely ever hear stories of an entire company being swallowed up by the earth in a single convulsion, never again to see the sun rise. The sea does that to ships in every season from what stories I have heard, and without any consideration for the caution and station of the men it takes for its own."

The other soldier conceded the point with a wave of his hand. "You are not wrong about that, and yet, whole mountains of men die upon the same little patch of land where they were born, never having seen beyond the brow of the next hill. How is it any better to to let *time* dash you against the walls of your small room, as you say?"

James grinned. "I suppose that I am better suited to let time destroy me at the end of a long and profitable life than to give the sea a chance to do so after a short and miserable career upon its face."

The other man returned his grin. "And I am more inclined to take the chance that the sea might offer me rewards in proportion to the risks that I find there." He glanced around to make sure that nobody was in earshot, and added in a lower voice, "I mean to sign up on one of those frigates just as soon as I can find one that will take me, but I haven't yet met the terms of my enlistment."

"Can you not serve out your enlistment as well on board a ship of the Continental navy as in a brigade of our army? I confess that I have never investigated the question, as I do not share your inclination toward the sea."

The other man shrugged. "I do not know the legal details, but neither do I care enough about them to let myself be entangled by them. When I get my chance, I will leap at it."

He lifted down the last crate of the captured supplies from the cart. "In any event, I need to return to the boat and fetch the next load of *gifts* our guests brought with them. The commander of the prize ship wants to start equipping it for our own purposes at once."

James sent him on his way with a cheery wave and a rueful shake of his head.

Men who needed the sort of adventure that this fellow craved had always been a mystery to him. After all, hadn't he seen plenty of the countryside, without ever stepping foot on a vessel any larger than a ferry across a river?

The risks of undertaking a lengthy voyage upon the sea were greater than he was willing to undertake, anyway. The fate of the enemy's horses bothered him in particular. What cruelty to place creatures meant for the stability and freedom of the open road into a cramped and storm-tossed ship. Worse, based on what the soldier had described, they were kept below decks, denied even fresh air. It sounded to him like an awful way for a man to live, never mind an animal that could not hope to understand the fate that had befallen it.

He stretched and dismissed the dismal thought, reminding himself that there was nothing that he could do for the horses, but that the supplies that had been confiscated and delivered here needed to be brought in out of the possibility of weather, and stored properly.

Unfortunately, the officer who had sent him out to meet the delivery clearly hadn't anticipated the weight of the cargo that would arrive.

James called out to a passing soldier, "Say, could you help me to bring this up into the storeroom? The fellow who delivered it could not stay to help."

The man grumbled, but ambled over, positioning himself on the other side of the crate. James did likewise, nodded sharply to him, and together, they lifted it up and began working their way to the gate of the fort, shuffling along with the load between them.

James never quite understood what happened, but the other man uttered a short shout of surprise, and fell heavily, the massive crate falling with its edge across both of his shins.

James heard a sharp crack even before the other soldier began to howl his pain, and once he'd recovered his own balance, he immediately set to lifting the crate off of the man's legs.

"Help!" he shouted to a knot of soldiers who were just coming out of the gate. They looked over to see him struggling and broke into a run, arriving to quickly remove the load from the fallen man and set it aside.

One man — an officer, James noticed — bent to examine the stricken man's legs. Even before the man's shoes and stockings were off, James knew his injuries were serious. He'd never *heard* bones break before, but he had no doubt at all about the source of the sound.

The injured man screamed as his stockings were pulled over the broken shins, and James winced.

"We must get this man to the hospital," said the officer, his expression grim.

James nodded, and said, "Help me lift him. Do you know where the hospital has been rigged up here in the fort?"

The other soldier nodded. "Aye, it's just behind the barracks."

He bent and started directing the rest of them to help. "Here, get his arm over your shoulder and join hands with me to carry him. You, help him up to sit on our hands."

He spoke to the injured man, who was now looking away from where his lower legs were bent the wrong direction. "What's your name, soldier?"

The man gasped, "Horatio— Hammond— sir."

"All right, Horatio, we'll get you to the surgeon straight away, and he'll get those legs splinted for you." To James, the man said, "Ready?"

James nodded, and with the help of the third man, they lifted the injured man up, and in relatively short order, had him inside the fort and around to where the surgeon had set up his hospital. The medical man had them set the patient on a raised table, and said, "Wait for a bit, as I will probably need your help with his treatment."

After examining Hammond, the doctor offered him a stiff tot of rum and, ominously, a leather strap. "Bite down upon this while I set those breaks. There's nothing to be done for it until I have the bones back in their right positions."

He directed James to stand at his patient's feet, and the other soldiers to keep him still on the table. "Do you think you can hold him, without we have strapped him down, or should we take the time to do that?"

The officer looked over the patient, who was of comparatively slight build, and said, "I reckon I can hold him down. You've got the harder job."

The doctor shook his head. "Nay, this poor fellow's got the harder job. All right, Mister Hammond. I'm going to tie a splint to the first leg, then we'll set the bones, and I'll secure the other end of the splint. Once that's done, I'll move to the other leg. Try to keep the strap between your teeth, so you do not do yourself further injury. I will not deceive you — this is going to hurt, probably more than the original injury did. Are you ready?"

Without waiting for an answer from the injured man, the doctor said to James, "You are to pull on his foot, while I guide the bones back to where they need to be. We are now fighting against his flesh, which will be trying to draw the broken parts out of all alignment, so you may need to use quite a bit of force. Just take comfort in the knowledge that you can hardly do him any more harm than he has already suffered."

James swallowed hard, and positioned himself by the whimpering patient's feet as the surgeon secured a splint on each side above the break on the first leg. Finishing the knots, the surgeon put his hands on the break and nodded emphatically to James.

The process was less awful than James had expected, in part because the patient let out a small squeak at the first touch and then fell silent, having fainted at the pain. James pulled his foot out straight at the surgeon's direction, and then held it in place until the splint was secured at the bottom end and the doctor declared himself satisfied.

They repeated the process with the other leg, except that the surgeon had to work the shin bone with his fingers for quite a while before it was in the position he wanted. Watching the process had James feeling as though he was going to join the patient in the dark precincts of unconsciousness by the time the doctor began tying the splints onto the man's second leg.

Finally, the surgeon wrapped both legs tightly with cloth, securing the splints and protecting the breaks within them, and then stepped back, shaking his head and letting out a gusty breath.

"Thank you, both, for bringing him in, and for helping me get him started. I am extremely short-handed here, particularly as the Negroes who were to be sent to help me were held back instead for the hospital in the city."

He turned to the officer who'd helped bring in the injured man. "Sir, can you contact Mister Hammond's commanding officer and inform him that his soldier will need to be sent back to the city to recover?"

The officer nodded briskly. The doctor now addressed James. "And are you at liberty to accompany Mister Hammond to the city? He will need someone to speak for him when he arrives, as he may not recover himself for some hours yet. I did him the favor of slipping some laudanum into his rum, but I can spare him no more from my stores."

James shook off the faintness that was still hovering around his mind at witnessing the grotesque process of setting bones, and answered, "If you can but send word to Sergeant Borland, I am certain I can undertake that duty."

He felt a certain level of responsibility for Hammond's injury, even though it had been purely an accident.

The doctor nodded curtly. "I will call for a wagon, and send word ahead that you will need a boat. I leave Private Hammond in your care until you can deliver him to the main hospital of this army."

Chapter 20

The trip across the harbor was no more eventful than any other ferry crossing James had been on, but the added burden of responsibility for the unconscious Hammond beside him combined with his reflections on the fate of the British horses to raise his anxiety to new heights, until the flat-bottomed boat scraped up on the shore, far from the Charles-Town quay.

James looked up sharply, and asked, "Weren't we to go to the city?"

One of the boatmen answered gruffly over his shoulder, "No, the hospital's at a barracks out on this side of town. Don't you worry none, we know our way around this place."

His declaration was punctuated by a chuckle by the other boatmen.

They'd done their best to adhere to the doctor's admonition to row in such a way as to avoid jarring his patient, rather than indulging in their favorite game of tormenting any landsman whose fear they could detect.

Upon their arrival, their leader called up to a watchman on the shore, "We've a hurt man here, and need a wagon to transport him to hospital immediately."

The watchman nodded and trotted off to summon a drover.

Blissfully unaware of the temptation that the boatmen had resisted, James had only noticed their solicitous treatment of Private

Hammond's transportation.

As he accepted the hand offered by one of the boatmen to step out of the boat onto the sandy shore, he said, solemnly, "I thank you on the patient's behalf, and mine, for your swift and careful service."

The boatman nodded his acknowledgment of James' gratitude, and turned to the job of lifting Hammond's litter out of the boat and up onto the shore. James stepped forward and took his place at one corner of the litter, and helped to carry the injured man up to where a wagon had already rumbled up for their use.

The ride to the hospital over the hard-packed dirt roads, which presently gave way to cobbled streets was gentle enough by normal standards, but even in his laudanum-induced stupor, Hammond groaned and struggled as the cart bumped along. James rested a hand on the patient's chest, saying, "You keep still now. We're almost to the hospital, and there you can rest and let those bones knit up."

In truth, he had no idea how far the hospital was. He was relying entirely on the drover to deliver them with all possible speed and care. The old nag who drew the cart seemed disinclined to speed, but at least she was also disinclined to cut capers or jump in reaction to surprises along the way.

After what seemed like hours of turns and bumps, the drover bade his old horse to stop, and turned around to his passengers. "The hospital's just inside there. I will stay with your man if you like while you go and fetch assistants to carry him in." He gestured just off the road toward a trio of brick buildings arranged about a central courtyard.

James gave the man a puzzled look. "Do you not think that

we could handle him, just the two of us, for that little distance?"

The drover's expression turned briefly inscrutable, but he shook his head. "Nay, it wouldn't be prudent. They don't like to have people from the town in there any more than strictly necessary, don't you know?"

James didn't know, but he sighed and bent to the inevitable. "Very well, then. I will return in a moment."

He slid down off the side of the wagon and approached the courtyard, looking to see if he could spot any guard or other soldiers about. A tall figure emerged from the nearest building, clad in the uniform of the regiment of *Chasseurs-Volontaires*, and James cried out in recognition.

He hailed the Frenchman at the top of his lungs, "Claude!" The soldier spun around at hearing his name and his face lit up in joy. Claude dashed toward James, speaking in rapid-fire French, and then gathered him into a quick embrace of greeting.

James returned the embrace, but said, "My friend, I am sorry, but I still have not learned any of the French, so you must bring me to someone who can translate for us."

Pointing to the wagon, he added, "But first, we need men to help carry this injured soldier." He mimed carrying the litter with his hands, and Claude nodded, moving toward the wagon.

Even without any shared words, the two were able to lift Hammond's litter, and James called out over his shoulder to the drover, "Thank you, sir, for your care in bringing us here!"

The man gave him a wave, already twitching the reins with his other hand to urge his horse into motion.

James let Claude lead the way as he carried the front of the litter, trusting that he would know where a new patient should be delivered. For his part, he focused on placing his feet, to avoid repeating the misstep that had led to Hammond's injury.

Inside the building, they maneuvered the litter to set it upon a low table, and Claude called out to someone in the next room. A man bustled into the room after a short delay, his manner harried and the bags visible under his eyes testified to the overwhelming amount of work he faced, unmistakably marking him as a medical man.

Seeing the man on the litter, the medic sighed gustily and looked Hammond over quickly. "Broken leg— no, *both* legs? How on the wide green world did he contrive to break them both at once? Never mind, follow me to the ward and bring him with you. What did you say his name is?"

This last was tossed over his shoulder as he hurried back through the door by which he'd entered. Claude was already positioning himself at the head of the litter, and James gave him a questioning look, wishing he could ask if this doctor's speech was always so rapid-fire.

The French soldier just grinned and took the end of the litter in his hands, tipping his head toward the now-empty doorway to indicate that they should follow the doctor.

James hurriedly bent to take up his end of the litter and called after the doctor, "I didn't get a chance to yet, sir. But his name is Private Horatio Hammond, and he fell while carrying supplies captured from the British. The crate caught his legs and broke both of them."

He maneuvered the litter through the doorway in time to hear the doctor's bark of laughter. "So, even in defeat, the enemy has arranged for his cargo to carry on the war, eh? That's a new tactic, but even though it seems like an inefficient way to reduce our forces. But it appears to have worked well enough in this fellow's case, eh? This way, keep up with me."

James, replied, "Aye, sir. The doctor out at the fort set the bones, and dosed Private Hammond with some laudanum, but he said that you would be better equipped to care for him than we are."

The doctor turned his head long enough to fix James with a frown, and shot back, "He did, eh? Nice for him to make that determination without consulting me, but in this case, I suppose he wasn't wrong."

He gestured them forward. "Just in here, if you please. This man will be a while healing enough to hobble about, if he can ever walk properly again. It all depends upon how the bones were broken, and how well they are set."

He led them into a long room with one long wall pierced with windows at regular intervals. The only furnishing was a row of beds, most of which were already occupied with convalescents of varying degrees of wakefulness, ranging from men who sat up with alert eyes taking in the new arrival, to those who lay unconscious and unresponsive.

"There you go," the doctor directed them, to an empty bed that sat between a man who lay with his eyes wide open to the ceiling, and one who was curled up on his side, groaning at the disturbance.

The staring man blinked as James looked at him, else he might have thought the poor soul already dead.

Claude maneuvered the head of the litter to lay it on the bed, and James followed suit with the other end. The French soldier was already working to lift Hammond and shift him over, so the doctor stepped in to help transfer him.

He said sharply to James, "You, move his hips onto the bed. I'll take his feet, as they cannot bear any weight. There, yes, just like that, and . . . *now.*"

James was impressed at how naturally Claude seemed to know what was needed, even without being able to understand the doctor's instructions.

In another moment, the doctor and his assistant were pulling the litter out from under their patient and setting it alongside the bed.

"Very good. Now that you've delivered your patient, you are free to go . . . sorry, I didn't get your name."

"Private Hatch, sir. But—"

"Good, thank you, Hatch. Have a safe journey back to the fort." He turned to leave.

"Just a moment, sir." James motioned toward Claude. "This man is a friend of mine, from our service together at Savannah, and I have not had a chance to speak with him in over a month. Is there anyone here who you could spare for a few minutes to act as a translator for us, so that we can at least exchange greetings before our duties again separate us?"

The doctor stopped, looking startled. "Oh, you say you know this fellow? That's a great coincidence. Of course I should be happy to spare him for a few minutes."

He cast about, looking at the other men working in the ward.

"Let me see, Alexandre over there has pretty good English." He called out, "Alexandre, come here, if you could."

One of the *Chasseurs-Volontaires* looked up sharply and approached at a brisk pace. James thought to himself that everyone here seemed to be perpetually in a hurry, and guessed that it was a reflection of the doctor's manner.

The Frenchman arrived and said, "Yes, Doctor Ashford?"

"Will you replace the bandages on Corporal McRae's wound, and help your countryman to communicate with this soldier? They know each other already, and desire to renew their acquaintance." Without waiting for an answer, the doctor turned and hurried away.

Alexandre smiled at the medic's retreating form. "Yes, doctor, with pleasure." He turned to Claude and shot a quick, questioning phrase at him in French.

Claude answered, and Alexandre turned to James, "He says that you look well, for all that he has heard that your company has been employed in heavy work these many weeks."

James nodded. "It is true that we have been ill-used, but if it means that we can hold off the enemy if they attempt to take this place, it will have been well worth the work. Have you all been kept busy since our arrival?"

The question was directed at Claude, but Alexandre answered at once, without consulting Claude, "We cannot complain. There are always cases who need tending to. The usual camp fevers, injuries such as this man's, and the men who are still recovering from their wounds at Savannah..." He indicated the staring man with his eyes, but said nothing beyond that.

He made his way to the staring man's side, and flipped down the blanket that covered the patient's torso, speaking in French to Claude as he simultaneously attended to his medical duties. With practiced hands, he lifted away the bloodstained bandage that lay over the man's abdomen, and reached into his pocket for a fresh bandage, quickly covering the angry-looking, ulcerated hole in the man's belly.

Covering the patient up with his blanket again and switching back to English, he relayed to James, "Claude says that he should be happier to be bound back for home, as it is entirely too cold here for his tastes, but he is pleased enough to be of some use. This work, for all that it can be distressing" — he motioned with his chin to the staring man, whose blank expression had not changed throughout the entire operation — "is, at least, not otherwise particularly demanding."

The patient on the other side of Hammond's bed stirred and moaned aloud, and Alexandre went to his side. He laid a hand on the man's cheek, but snatched it back, looking suddenly concerned. James watched as he gingerly pulled the man's blanket back and opened his shirt.

Alexandre's countenance grew suddenly very serious, and he tucked the blanket back down quickly. He turned to James and said, firmly, "Stay right here. I will be back immediately." He spoke to Claude in the same tone, presumably giving the French soldier a similar admonition.

James was puzzled, but he did not become alarmed until he saw Alexandre break into a run as he left the room. What had he seen on the groaning man's chest that could have elicited such a reaction?

He did not have long to wonder, as the doctor returned with Alexandre at an even faster pace than he had left. He turned down the blanket, peering at the man's chest, and then nodded, sighing. "You are correct, Alexandre. It is the pox."

He looked up at James and Claude, and said to James, "My sincere apologies, Private . . . Hatch, was it? I don't suppose by any chance that you have been inoculated under General Washington's orders . . . or are you a militiaman?"

James shook his head, bewildered and frightened. "I originally joined a militia, but transferred to a Continental unit after we arrived at Savannah. So . . . I have not been inoculated, no."

The doctor nodded briskly. "Then I must insist that you stay here in quarantine for no less than a fortnight, lest you inadvertently bring the contagion back with you to the fort. Your commanders will not object, as few things strike more fear into the heart of a general who may be on the eve of battle than to hear that his troops have been exposed to the smallpox."

Chapter 21

James didn't know what was worse — watching the three men around him who had turned out already to be infected suffer the agonies of the pox, or waiting to learn whether he would join them. The first man on whom it had been detected had progressed from moaning occasionally, to shouting his agony throughout the night.

The man with the stomach wound, who'd done nothing but stare at the ceiling as the medics treated him, never said anything, but as his fever rose, his gaze slowly went from being empty to completely still, until he finally took one deep, shuddering breath, and then sighed his last.

The other man who had entered quarantine with James and Horatio was the soldier who'd been in the bed to the other side of the first case. James never did learn that man's name. Originally in the hospital for the flux, he had outlasted the silent man by only a few hours. The fever had taken him just as the first pox were starting to form on his face.

The doctor had shaken his head, frowning, as he drew the man's blanket over his head to cover it.

"Two in one day, out of three cases, is more than we usually lose to the pox, but neither of these men were in any shape to fight the disease, either." He gave James and Horatio what James supposed was meant to be a reassuring smile. "You both are healthy, so there is little for you to fear."

He hurried out then, sending Alexandre and Claude in again to remove the corpse. They had been tending to all of the men in the pox ward, as Doctor Ashford had ordered that only those who had undergone the inoculation procedure or already survived the pox could enter the room. He'd said, briskly, displaying a small, puckered scar on his hand, "I've had the inoculation, of course, and Alexandre tells me that both he and Claude were exposed as children and recovered."

So it was that the two French soldiers came in and efficiently removed the dead man, wrapping him in his blanket and removing him with all of his bedding, to be buried or perhaps burned — James wasn't sure which, and he didn't want to ask, lest it haunt his already vivid nightmares.

He and Horatio had a grim wager between them as to which of them would fall ill first. Horatio had awoken from his laudanum-enhanced dreams to find himself in the isolated ward, with only James and the three sick men around him. James had explained the situation, and Horatio had rolled away and refused to speak with him.

James had tried to apologize to the man — after all, he did feel a degree of responsibility for his accident — but Horatio had refused to answer or acknowledge him for an hour or more. Eventually, though, the moans of the man furthest along in his infection had driven him to roll back toward James, who sat quietly on his bed, pondering the fickleness of fate.

Horatio said, abruptly, "I cannot die this way. I will not stand for it. I could bear for my mama to get word that an enemy bullet had carried me away, and that I went to my maker fighting for the independence of our country, but for her to have a letter from someone telling her that the accursed *pox* got me? Unthinkable."

James answered, "At least your parents would be glad to hear that your death was in the service of the fight against the British. I rather suspect that mine would think that I got what I deserved." James wasn't sure when this realization had broken over him, but it felt good to finally confess it out loud to someone.

After a shocked silence, Horatio finally said, "Better that we both live, then, I to be able to carry word of my heroism home, and you as rebuke when this matter is concluded. What do you say, shall we swear on it?"

James smiled and shook his head at being asked to swear yet another oath. "Sure," he said easily, "If by swearing on it we can ward off the bad humors that gather around us in this place, I will swear on my grandfather's name that I will live to return home and convince my parents that I fought on the side of the right, and that they should be proud of me."

Horatio grinned and held out his hand to shake James'. The other man winced as they shook, though, and remarked, "I am not permitted to forget for a moment that my legs lie in pieces within my bandages, am I?"

James nodded in sympathetic acknowledgment, and Horatio looked around them at the other three men. "None of our companions here are insensate enough that they are not suffering from whatever brought them here in the first place . . . so I have that much to look forward to, I suppose."

He asked in a low enough tone that only James could hear, "They're not much company, are they?"

"No, not at all," James agreed at a similar volume, and told

Horatio what he knew of each of their histories. Horatio grimaced when James described the stomach wound that the silent man bore, and frowned at the description of the pox on the chest of the moaning man.

But instead of inquiring further about the other patients, Horatio glanced around to ensure that nobody else had come into the ward — James thought it a funny sort of gesture — and leaned closer. "I don't suppose you have any dice with you?"

James shook his head. "I have never played at dice." He didn't add that he had avoided the inevitable late-night games around the various encampments in part because his father had always hinted to him that men who played at dice were low and untrustworthy, liable to leave their debts unpaid.

However, he was feeling rebellious against his father's guidance at the moment, so when Horatio reached into his pocket and drew forth a handful of the marked cubes, he did not recoil, but instead leaned in closer to examine them.

"Made these myself just last week," Horatio commented, passing them over. "The cook had some beef bones left over that I persuaded him to let me have, instead of tossing them to the dogs. I've given them a good go, and they seem to throw true."

James shot him a puzzled look, and Horatio explained, "None of them seem to favor any side over another, so they offer a fair chance of landing on any of the six. You can tell which side is which by the pips I burned into them."

James rolled the dice around in his hand, and remarked, "They are neat work, to be sure, but is it worth the risk to have them loose in your pocket like that? You know that throwing dice is against the law of the army."

Horatio grinned and held out his hand for James to return the dice. "Why do you think I had to make fresh ones so recently? A lieutenant from another company surprised me, coming around a corner quiet like a cat, and took my old ones. My own lieutenant would have looked the other way, but this fellow was a right stickler about the regulations."

He snorted, adding, "Or else he wanted some bones of his own to throw in the officers' games. I didn't see him put them in the fire, as he might have done straightaway, if he'd wanted them truly destroyed."

Horatio gave James a speculative look. "So, do you want to learn how to play a couple of games with 'em? Just to pass the time, since we're stuck here, and liable to be left in peace for quite a while."

James nodded, but warned, "I have no wealth to offer you, so we shall have to play for fun only, rather than money."

Horatio shrugged. "Have it your way, but I find that nothing sharpens the fun of the game like having a little bit of blood in it." He grinned. "But I'll teach you to play for points, and you can decide if it would be more entertaining to put a value on those points later, all right?"

James agreed, "Sounds good to me."

Horatio nodded, a wide grin on his face, and James was glad that he had found something with which to distract his mind from the pain of his broken legs and the uncertainty of their fates in the pox ward.

"We'll start with an easy game — pair and ace. We'll each cast one die to determine whose turn is first." He handed James a die, and motioned to the tin plate that sat at the foot of James' bed, left from his breakfast of bread and cheese. "That will work as a flat surface on which to cast, though it will be noisier than I'd like."

He shook the die in his own hand, blowing into the side of his clenched fist — "For luck," he explained — and motioned for James to do likewise.

It took James a moment to get the hang of leaving enough room inside his fist for the die to move freely, while not leaving any gaps where it might fly out. He did not relish the prospect of trying to find the small cubes amongst the folds of his bedding, so he erred at first on the side of caution.

Horatio motioned toward the plate with a sharp nod, and James managed to release his die at the same time as the other man's, the carved bones making a sharp rattling noise on the metal surface. Horatio examined the dice and said, "I have rolled a five, while you got an ace — just one pip — so you'll go first."

He gathered up his own die and handed James two others, along with the one remaining on the plate. "Now, we take turns casting three dice all together, until one of us comes up with an ace and two matching numbers — a pair — on the remaining two dice. So, 'pair and ace,' do you smoke it?"

He smiled again, and James couldn't help but grin in reply. "And that person is the winner?"

"Aye, and if we are playing for points, we'll keep track of the pairs we roll and add those to our tally."

James nodded. "That seems easy enough." He gave his dice a good shake, blowing into his hand for good measure, and cast them onto the plate.

Horatio chortled, "You very nearly won it on the first cast, friend. You again rolled an ace, but you missed the pair." James peered down at the dice, which showed six pips on one and two on the other, and scooped them up from the plate.

Horatio gave his dice a quick shake and cast them, coming up with a pair of fives, but a six where he needed the ace. He shook his head ruefully and gathered his dice up again.

They continued back and forth for what seemed like endless rounds, often coming up with a pair *or* an ace, but not both together, until James finally cast a pair of sixes and an ace, and Horatio exclaimed for victory.

James chortled and grabbed the dice, saying, "Surely that game sometimes goes more quickly, though?"

Horatio shrugged. "It's all in the luck of the throw. I've watched men lose their entire back pay on it, though, doubling and redoubling their wagers with each throw." He winked broadly. "As I said, some blood in the game makes it much more exciting."

"I am sure that it would be exciting for you, but as for myself, I would doubtless only lose *my* back pay, which would be far less exciting from my side of the plate."

Horatio laughed loudly enough now that the man behind him — the first pox sufferer — woke up and groaned, "Can't you two take your accursed throwing of lots and tin-plate rattling and laughing *outside*, so that a man can get some rest for his aching head?"

"No, we cannot," Horatio answered, impatiently. "On account of having been nearby when you broke out in the pox, we are all five obliged to stay shut up in here until we have all died of it, or else wished that we had."

James added, in a more mollifying tone, "We will endeavor, though, to be less noisy for your comfort." To Horatio, he said quietly, "The time may well come when we are the ones cursing at boisterous company. It's not his fault, if we do come down with the pox ourselves."

Horatio grumbled, "Not only that, but I don't know how the doctor would feel about his patients throwing dice, and this fellow could get us both in trouble, were he to mention it." He motioned toward the plate. "Wish we had a quieter surface on which to cast."

James suggested, "Let me look around and see what there might be. If nothing else, I can drag a table over to stand between our beds, and tell the doctor I wanted to eat sitting up, like a civilized man."

Horatio gestured at his legs, under the blankets, and snorted, "I suppose that makes me a savage, then?" However, he tempered his bitter words with a smile, and waved a dismissive hand at James. "Go on, then, see what you can find."

James came back with a wooden tray that he found sitting atop a stool.

"That is perfect," Horatio decided. "It should bother our friend a lot less, and the sides will contain the dice better, too. Now, since you won the last round, I'll go first this time."

He cast a winning throw on the first attempt, and had to silence himself before he disturbed the ill man behind him again. When he'd mastered himself, he told James, "Go on, then, your turn to start us off."

They played a dozen or more rounds, and then Horatio said, "Now, here's another game, called Riffa. Same basic idea, except we each throw three dice until we get a pair, and then roll the third one to determine our total score. I like to play this one at a penny for ten, if I'm playing for money."

"A penny for ten?"

"Oh, aye, a penny for each ten points won, and settle up at the end of the game. But for now, we'll still just play for fun, eh?"

"Sure,"

James rolled until a pair of fives appeared, and then rolled a six to join them.

Horatio laughed. "I think I'm happier that we're not playing for money, else I'd owe you nearly the price of a loaf of bread already."

The afternoon passed by quickly enough, with James learning the basics of *rounds*, *both-in-one*, and failing utterly to grasp a complex game that Horatio called "*hazards*." That last involved an inherent aspect of wagering that made James' head spin.

James could see that Horatio was becoming weary, as he had become quite impatient when trying to explain hazards to him.

"It's not that complicated. If I roll a main of seven, and then throw in with a seven or an eleven, I win the round, while a twelve will lose, as will either a two or a three, of course, which always loses. If my main is a six or an eight, rolling a matching six or eight will win, will a twelve, while an eleven will lose, along with two or three. Five and nine are the hardest to win, as you must nick with the same roll, and—"

James interrupted him. "Can we just stick with both-in-one? I like that one. We can play for a penny in ten, if you like, as I feel ready for some small wagers."

Horatio nodded, chewing on the inside of his mouth as he considered. Finally, he said, "Very well. Let's start at a penny in a hundred, just so that neither one of us needs to go without bread tomorrow."

He was jesting, of course, as either Alexandre or Claude brought them bread every afternoon, at the doctor's expense. He seemed to believe that it was a preventative to the onset of the pox, and neither James nor Horatio were inclined to argue with him.

James enjoyed the fact that this game required him to quickly add up the two smaller numbers to see if they added up to the larger one thrown. The points were only scored from the largest number, and between keeping track of that, and the constant exercise of addition of the dice thrown, it was the game that had held his attention for the longest.

They took turns throwing, and James soon found the rhythm of it nearly as soothing and compelling as a long march in step, the jangle of the dice in hand and the comforting patter as they struck the tray lulling him into a state of not quite sleep, but not quite full wakefulness.

After a hour or so, Horatio owed James just less than two pence, when he finally leaned back and said, "I am tired, my friend, and I should rest, to give my legs a chance to knit properly."

James answered, "Of course," and handed the dice over to the other man, who dropped them into his pocket and drew the strings to shut it tightly. He settled back on his bed, closing his eyes and appearing as though he had fallen asleep already.

"What do you want to wager on which of us will fall ill with the pox first," Horatio asked, suddenly, his eyes still closed.

The idea struck James as morbid, but he tried to laugh off his discomfort. "I don't know . . . perhaps double or nothing on what you owe from our game?"

Horatio opened his eyes and grinned at James. "I thought you said you were not a gambling man?" He closed his eyes once more. "It's a wager, then, but we'll round it to two pence, either way. Does that suit you?"

James nodded, then realized that the other man could not see the gesture, and said aloud, "That suits me, though I'll be happiest if neither of us needs to collect on this particular wager."

Horatio chuckled. "Well, I cannot argue with you on that."

A few days later, just after the second man in the pox ward had succumbed, Horatio called over to James, "Well, friend, I feel a fever coming on, and I do not know that I will be able to keep my breakfast down. I think that you have won our little wager."

Chapter 22

Although Horatio had manifested the symptoms first, James was not far behind him. It started with the prickling hot sensation of a rising fever, felt in his eyes, and he quickly learned why the first man infected had been moaning so loudly, as his back was seized with spasms of pain.

Beside him, Horatio seemed to be having a somewhat easier time of it, merely looking listless and feverish, but not complaining of the backaches or even the pounding head that had wracked their other companion. That man was now sitting upright in his bed, the pox across his face having already ruptured and started to form scabs.

In his more lucid moments, James thought the man looked closer to death than ever, but he was clearly feeling better, no matter how horrific his appearance might be. He'd called over that afternoon, "I have gathered from listening to you two converse that one of you is called Horatio, and the other is James. I am Justin Ford, private soldier in the South-Carolina militia."

James and Horatio both mumbled their greetings, although James could not understand why the man was so chipper. He'd heard Doctor Ashford comment on his high fever, and cluck sympathetically at the man's open pox.

James mustered the energy to ask Justin, "How is it that you are sicker than both of us, yet you are sitting upright, while we are laid low?"

Justin chuckled. "Why, isn't it perfectly obvious? I have come far enough through the course of the illness that I may be quite certain of surviving it, and will never again need to fear the pox. My chest is on fire, but my soul is singing." James groaned and rolled over to face away from the recovering soldier.

The next morning, Justin's soul had ceased singing, at least in the precincts of life on earth. When Alexandre came in to change their beds, he jumped back on touching Justin's shoulder. Hearing the French man's gasp, James asked, groggily, "What is the matter?"

"Oh, this man has gone on ahead of us to meet his maker." Alexandre's tone was mournful. "And he seemed to be doing so well, too. Doctor Ashford will be terribly disappointed that his treatment did not save this man."

He looked sharply over at James, reassuring him, "Have faith, though, as I have seen the good doctor bring some men back from the very edge of the hereafter. He is better-educated on every aspect of modern medical practice than any other I have seen, and he has a great many creative ideas of his own, as well."

Then he sighed, and said, "I must go and ask Claude to help me carry this unfortunate fellow out with his things to consign to the fire."

James frowned, not trusting his stomach enough to open his mouth to speak.

He had the answer to his curiosity about the fate of those who died in this ward, but he could not say it provided him any comfort.

Not that it would make any difference to his parents, he

reflected bitterly, whether his body were consigned to the damp and heavy clay here, or turned to ash.

Having now watched every one of the men who had been ill when they'd entered the pox ward exit it in a winding sheet, James had little hope that he would do otherwise, no matter how much confidence Alexandre had in the doctor.

Horatio groaned and rolled toward James, looking at him with dull eyes. He took a labored breath and asked, "We're going to die, aren't we?"

James shook his head. "You heard what Alexandre said. The doctor knows all of the latest and best treatments, and we both have the advantage of having entered this ward in strong health."

"What of Private Ford, there?"

"He must have been in hospital for something else."

Their further musings were interrupted as Doctor Ashford came in at an uncharacteristically moderate pace, his shoulders slumped. He was trailed by Alexandre and Claude, who stopped and waited by the door as the doctor went over to examine Ford's corpse.

The doctor pulled back Ford's blanket, and James wished that he had been turned to face the other way. The blanket stuck to Ford's body where the pox had seeped into the fabric, so the doctor had to pull it quite briskly to free it. Shaking his head, he bent and looked more closely at Ford's face, finally standing up and pulling the blanket up to cover the unfortunate man's body.

He waved to Alexandre. "You may take him away. It is as I'd feared. The pox took hold in his mouth, and I am quite confident that they closed up his throat, and eventually robbed him of his breath. The disease progresses with shocking speed in such an instance."

James was emboldened enough by this pronouncement to ask, "And how long until the same happens to us?"

The doctor appeared to be startled by his question. "How's that again? Oh, no, you two are wholly different cases, as Ford came in after a snakebite had already nearly suffocated him. No, I expect both of you to make full recoveries in time."

James gave him a skeptical look, and the doctor smiled grimly. "Not that it will be a pleasant course. I won't lie to you . . . over the next few weeks, you will likely be as sick as you will ever be in your life, but at the end of it, you will emerge. Perhaps you will not be so pretty as you are now, but I have no doubt at all that you will both be fine."

His reassurance came as little comfort to either James or Horatio as they suffered through the following few days of illness.

However, the morning came when Horatio awoke and called out to James, "I do believe that doctor was on to something when he said we would be all right. I have hardly felt so well since I arrived in this wretched state."

James groaned and rolled over. "Bully for you," he mumbled irritably.

The illness seemed to have taken up residence inside his skull, and wanted out something powerful, pounding and pressing so hard that James expected his head to simply explode. However, he had to admit — once he'd had his bread and cheese — that he, too, was feeling less like he *wanted* to die, and more just as though he *would* die. It was a marginal improvement, but it was there.

After Claude had come around to take away their dishes, James realized that his headache was mostly gone, so he sat up and asked, "Do you feel up to some both-in-one, if only to take our minds off of our miserable state?"

Horatio gave him a half-smile. "That is the entire reason to throw dice, my friend, no matter the state of your health." He nodded. "Perhaps a few throws of that, and then I can try to teach you to play farkle. It's an easier game than hazards, I'll wager."

James shot him a sardonic smile. "Is there anything you won't wager on?"

Horatio grinned widely. "Not that I've found yet. Here, let us cast to see who will take the first throw." They played for a while, not really keeping close track of the points, and then Horatio asked, "Are you ready to try something new?"

"Sure, I know you've been eager to show me this other game — barky, did you call it?"

"Farkle," Horatio corrected, with a grin. He looked around the ward, as though searching for something. "Have you seen a hornbook or even some scrap paper? The scoring for this game practically requires the use of such."

James frowned, shaking his head. "I have not, and I would rather not get up out of bed without Alexandre here to fetch the doctor, should I fall down. I feel weak enough to pass out in the attempt."

Horatio waved a dismissive hand. "No matter, we can ask Alexandre to bring something the next time he comes in. In the meantime, I can acquaint you with the rules."

Horatio began to lay out the basic idea of the game, turning and pulling more dice out of his pocket in order to do so. "You start out with a cast of six dice," he said, throwing a handful of dice onto the tray.

"The goal is to reach at least five hundred points in your turn."

James shot Horatio a half-smile. "You make it sound so simple. Can I just start counting now?"

Horatio smirked, but ignored him. "If you cast any five, that's worth fifty points. A single ace is one hundred points. Three aces are worth three hundred, three twos are worth two hundred, and three threes are again worth three hundred. We proceed in that way up to three sixes, which are worth six hundred points. Clear so far?"

"I suppose," James said, although all of the numbers were making his head ache again.

"Good, because now it gets a little more complicated. Four of a kind are worth one thousand points, five of a kind two thousand, and six of a kind, three thousand."

"I should think that they are worth that much, as rarely as you might roll them."

Horatio held up a finger. "We'll get to that in a moment, but first, there are a couple of other combinations worth points, as well. A run from ace to six is worth one thousand five hundred points, as are three pairs, or four of a kind and a pair. Finally, two sets of three of a kind are worth two thousand five hundred points."

James favored Horatio with a doubtful expression. "And you expect I can remember that, without it being written down."

"We'll write it down, if you need, but you'll find that it comes quite naturally with time. Now, as you pointed out, many of these combinations are almost impossible to throw on a single cast, so you can choose to build up to them."

James sighed and restrained himself from rolling his eyes,

but Horatio pressed on, undiscouraged. "Say you rolled three twos with your first throw. You could take the two hundred points and put them toward your turn total, or you could re-roll the other three and see whether you could either add to the three of a kind, or else roll another three of a kind."

"And if I fail to do that, I just keep the three of a kind?"

"No, if you re-roll any dice and they do not add to the value of the turn, you forfeit your turn, and none of what you've earned will go to your total. Remember, though, that if any of those three dice you're thinking about re-rolling come up as either an ace or a five, or a two of course, that will keep your turn alive."

"All right, but if I didn't re-roll any of them, my turn is only worth . . . two hundred now, am I recalling that correctly?"

"Yes, but since you haven't yet reached five hundred, it doesn't go to your total, so there's nothing lost in re-rolling those three, and everything to gain."

"Ah, I understand that necessity now." But it was completely clear to James that he did not understand very much else about the game, as he tried to remember the values of the combinations.

"So, let us say that you re-rolled the remaining three dice, and one of those came up as a two. That gives you four of a kind, worth how many points?"

James ventured, "Two thousand points?"

"No, that's five of a kind. Four of a kind is worth one thousand points, which is enough for you to add to your total and end your turn. Now, just for the sake of understanding what is possible, let us say that your re-roll of the three dice came up all twos, giving you six of a kind and three thousand points. You could take the points and end your turn, or, because you've now used all six dice to score, you can re-roll all six and try to keep adding to the value of your turn."

James shook his head. "I cannot imagine a circumstance in which I would want to do that, risking three thousand points!"

Horatio nodded. "That is a wise position, but there is one case where you would definitely want to press your luck. Once one player has passed a total of ten thousand points, everyone else at the table gets one last turn to see if they can exceed that player's score. So if you had three thousand points — or had managed to use all six dice to score something less — but it wasn't enough to top the other players' final scores, again, you'd have nothing to lose by continuing."

James thought this through. "I can see why you like this game even more than the others, as it lets you make little wagers at every move. I cannot say that it offers the same appeal to me, but I am willing to play, providing that we can write down those scoring rules, and keep track of our scores on a page of some sort."

"When Alexandre comes back, we'll see about that. In the meantime, would you like to cast a few practice rounds, to get a feel for it?"

"I suppose, although if my head starts to hurt again, I will need to lie down and let it rest."

"That's fair. Now, for this game, we determine who goes first by rolling a single die, with the highest roll playing first..."

By the time Alexandre came in to refresh the beds and deliver their supper, James was feeling more at ease with the complicated scoring and the calculation of risk versus reward, but he still wanted to ask for writing tools. Alexandre, though, seemed preoccupied and hurried.

When the French soldier nearly dropped his supper, James finally asked, "What is the matter with you this evening, Alexandre? I have never seen you in such a state."

Alexandre grimaced and looked toward the door. "I do not know whether the doctor meant for me to relay the news to you, or to let you recover in peace, but since you have asked, I will tell you."

He let his gaze fall upon the window where the evening sunlight shone in low over the landscape. "The enemy have landed an entire army just south of the city, and will doubtless come to reduce this place, just as quickly as they can."

Chapter 23

James didn't know if it was the bad news or simple bad fortune, but the next morning, his throat and the inside of his nose burned as though a fire were lit within them.

Describing this agony to Horatio, James was unsurprised to hear the other man say, "Aye, and I can feel bumps inside my mouth that feel the same way."

Doctor Ashford came in to check on them, and nodded sympathetically. "This is the normal progression of the disease, I am sorry to tell you. First in the mouth and throat or nose. By tomorrow, you will start to develop the pox proper, and all I can do to try to assure your recovery is to have the men bring you plenty to drink, and what broths you can stand to eat."

He laid his hand on James' chest, offering some measure of comfort. "When your throat is on fire, the best thing we can do is to try to quench that fire. I will see how my supply of small beer is, and failing that, I'll dose you with a proper naval grog, as I have plenty of rum laid in, and some sugar yet, as well."

He looked thoughtful and added, "In fact, I think I will start with the grog, as I suspect that it will be more soothing to your throat."

Turning to Horatio, the doctor said, "Let me see the back of your mouth, Mister Hammond."

Horatio obliged, opening as wide as he could, and sticking

his tongue out for the doctor to examine.

Satisfied, the doctor nodded for Horatio to go ahead and close his mouth again. "Yes, I think that will be just the thing. It's a pity I haven't any limes, to make it a truly naval drink, but it's probably just as well, since the juice of those might sharpen the soreness of your throats..."

He hurried out, still muttering to himself about naval medicine and the lessons it might offer even to a doctor of land soldiers. A short while later, Claude came in, carrying two tin cups full of what James presumed was the doctor's 'grog.'

After a taste, James decided he would have preferred the rum unspoiled by sweetening and thinning it, or the small beer that the doctor had mentioned in passing, but the drink did reduce the pain in his throat, and presently, he felt comfortable enough to return to sleep.

It seemed that Doctor Ashford was a good and capable physician, after all, and James dared to hope that he might yet recover from this new and unhappy phase of the dreaded disease.

When Alexandre came later with another cup of grog for each of the men, he also had a clear soup for their supper. By this time, though, the sores in Horatio's mouth caused him to cry out at the heat.

James sipped at his own broth, swallowing it painfully, and feeling bad for the other man's suffering.

The next fortnight was a steady progression of horrors for both men. As the doctor had predicted, the pox erupted across their faces, then appeared on their hands and arms. Over the following days, the red spots transformed into countless blisters, filled to bursting with liquid that was initially clear, but then turned cloudy.

And then, they began to rupture. James woke up in the middle of the night, feeling something wet running down his arm, and when he groggily tried to brush it off, he felt several other blisters burst and release their foul burdens onto his bedding.

Feeling suddenly nauseated, he froze, and very carefully laid back down, trying to ignore the pain from the now open sores on his arm. He realized that in reaching over to touch one arm, he had broken open some of the blisters on the other arm, as well, and had to swallow back the bile that rose at the back of his throat.

After what felt like a month of lying in the darkness, willing himself to be still and to pay no attention to the awful things happening to his body, James perceived that the sunrise was brightening the sky outside, and he dared to turn his head to face Horatio.

The other man lay quietly on his back, his mouth thrown open and emitting soft snores. James envied him briefly, but what remained of his reason reminded him that Horatio was doubtless in for the same terrible experience in the hours to come. There was no sense in resenting him for trailing James' progression in the course of the disease that was tormenting them both.

Eventually, Alexandre came in to check on them, and pursed his mouth sympathetically when James called out. "They're cracking open now."

The French soldier nodded. "I remember this part from when I had the pox as a boy. I wanted more than anything else to rub the blisters away, but to do so was agony." He paused, as if considering whether to go on, and then added, "The worst, though, is when there are so many of the pox open and running that you can smell them."

He shuddered in spite of himself, and again, James had to swallow his gorge.

From his bed, Horatio groaned and shifted. "I would build up a better appetite for my morning gruel without this conversation," he grumbled. "All the worse that it is but an advance look at what I have to expect of the days to come."

Alexandre dipped his head, a rueful expression on his face. "I should think that I would rather know what lies ahead in the progression of a disorder of my own body, but I should not have assumed the same on your behalf."

Horatio sighed. "No, you are right, of course. I suppose that it was waking up to this discussion that caused me the distress I felt."

James laughed, a brief, bitter sound, and said, "Be glad that you didn't wake up as I did, well before sunrise, to the sensation of the first of the blisters breaking open unbidden. I know not how I am expected to get any further sleep at all as this waking nightmare proceeds."

Without thinking about it, he shifted on his bed, and immediately winced, groaning, "Now I've gone and opened more of the pustules."

Alexandre rolled his head on his shoulders and said, "I will fetch the doctor presently to look in on you, but I know that he will want your clothes and blankets changed frequently as you endure this part of your ordeal. He has already made arrangements to have them boiled and dried only by those who have already had the pox, or those who happened to have been inoculated as he was."

He grimaced and said, "That will usually be me or Claude, of course. Although some of the other *Chasseurs-Volontaires* who are attached to the hospital also survived the pox in their childhoods, few of them trust the doctor's assurance that they cannot suffer it a second time."

Quietly, he added, "They think he's just willing to sacrifice them in the care of white men, and no matter how much I try to assure them that he cares for our health, too, they have been ill-used too many times to trust."

James shook his head, but could not think of anything to offer in comfort or sympathy. He was aware that the French soldiers had to labor under a set of circumstances and experiences that were utterly foreign to him, but it was always surprising to have that fact so inescapably put before him.

Alexandre squared his shoulders. "In any event, I will need to go and fetch clean bedding and clothing for you. Doctor Ashford is most determined that you do not suffer the fate of some men he has previously treated, whose skin became so attached to their blankets that it simply peeled off as he tried to turn them."

Horatio gulped audibly and turned pale, and Alexandre made a gesture of apology and hurriedly left, without adding anything else to the patients' discomfort.

The doctor entered shortly, looking worried and harried. "Alexandre informs me that the pox have begun to seep. There is little we need to change in your treatment with this development, but it is more important than ever that you continue to drink the naval grog or, if you prefer, small beer, in order to replenish the phlegmatic humor your body is expending in the seepage."

James said, "I think I should prefer to change to the small beer at this time, if you don't mind."

"Easily done. I anticipated that one or both of you might

like to make the exchange and have secured a cask for our medical uses here." He looked over to Horatio. "Should you like to make the same change, Private Hammond?"

"Nay, I have come to like the taste of the naval grog pretty well," Horatio said, a half-smile on his face. "I find, too, that I rest easier after I have taken it."

Doctor Ashford nodded, "It will have that effect, more so than the small beer."

He turned back to James. "The other necessity is that we must change your bedding as frequently as possible, lest it dry to your disrupted skin and cause further injury as you move about. While you endure this phase of the disease, there is little sense in clothing you otherwise, but we will dedicate a supply of fresh blankets to your purposes sufficient to give your bedding time to dry between washings."

James thought that the blankets would be less comfortable on his skin than the night shirt he had been wearing as his sole garment, but he did not argue the point. It was hard enough to ask those caring for him to continually wash his bedding, and he could not justify adding to their burdens. Never mind that he only owned the one night shirt anyway, so he would have had to acquire more of those to avoid the minor indignity of going naked for a time.

He nodded. "It seems sensible, though I am no Adam. I will welcome the return of my fig leaf, once I am fit enough to wear clothing again." He sighed. "If I should survive this disease, what else will it take from me besides my dignity and my boyish good looks?"

The doctor clasped his hands together. "As you say, the

pox will likely scar badly as they heal. You can help to reduce that by resisting the urge to scratch and pick at them, no matter how infernal the itching becomes."

"I will do my best, if only because I have no wife yet, and should like someday to find one."

The doctor rewarded James' witticism with a quick, sunny grin. "I will send Claude in to gather your bedding and clothes, and bring you fresh blankets. Do you need help getting up and pulling that shirt over your head?"

James shook his head and sat up, wincing as he felt his sleeves brush against the already opened blisters. He thought he could feel more bursting with even that slight movement. Gingerly moving the blanket aside, he swung his legs over the edge of the bed to rest on the floor, giving himself a moment to master his reaction to the many pains and discomforts of the motion.

Finally, he took a deep breath and lifted himself to a standing position, then gathered the hem of the night shirt and slowly drew it up over his head. He could feel where it clung to his arms as he went, and had to admit that he felt relief at no longer having the fabric close against his skin.

"Can you ask Claude to stoke the fireplace, as well?" he asked. "It is rather too cold in here to be standing about without any clothing at all."

"Of course. I will have Alexandre send him in immediately, and once you are back in bed, you and Mister Hammond can both break your fast."

He turned to go, then stopped for a moment. "I have every confidence that you both will recover, despite the hardships that lie before you."

After he left, Horatio uttered a brief, bitter chuckle. "At least I will not have to stand about clothed only in glory." James shot him a quick frown, and Horatio grinned, his visage all the more horrible for the blisters all over his face.

"I cannot yet stand, for one thing," he reasoned. "And even when the time comes that I, too, must abandon my garments, I will doubtless still need to have something about my legs to hold them while the bones knit."

James smiled in spite of himself. "You would find something to laugh about at the very gates to the Devil's abode," he said. "I am glad for that, but at the moment, I am too cold to do anything but wish that we were there already, if only for the warmth."

Chapter 24

James finally felt strong enough to join Horatio in taking in the spring air, performing slow turns around the hospital buildings. The other man's passage through the course of the disease had been relatively swift beginning with the dark days when pox had broken open, proceeding to form scabs everywhere, and eventually healed, leaving only a dense pattern of deep, puckered scars wherever they had been.

James, on the other hand, had developed infections in both legs that had seen his calves swell up like obscene balloons, bearing a crust of drying pox like the rind on an orange gone bad. His fever had risen to the point where he had a delirious memory of the doctor asking him one afternoon if he had any final wishes, or if he would like a letter prepared to send to his family.

Happily, however, the fever had broken that night, and the swelling in his legs had begun to reduce by the following night.

He had been as weak as a newborn colt the first time he'd tried to get out of bed, and it had been the work of long, patient hours with Alexandre and Doctor Ashford for him to regain even a shadow of his former strength.

Horatio, meanwhile, had started to move around on a pair of crutches that Doctor Ashford had procured for him, bearing most of his weight on his arms. He was able to take his first shaky, hesitant steps before James was even able to stand unassisted. Seeing his friend grin widely at being able to gingerly put one foot in front of the other reminded James to be thankful that he, at least, could put weight on his legs without worry.

As it was, he was grateful for the cane that Alexandre pressed into his hand, and he trailed along behind Horatio, feeling so weakened by the effort that he could scarcely do more than grunt in acknowledgment of the other man's words.

"I don't know whether you'd heard from Doctor Ashford of the affair at Monk's Corner," Horatio said.

When James shook his head in reply, the other man went on, "Oh, it was a shocking loss for our cause, and has put our position here in town in grave question. Why, Doctor Ashford told me that he'd even heard that the governor has fled the city."

James stopped walking and leaned heavily on the cane, feeling unaccountably light-headed. "Are things truly at so grim a pass for this garrison, then?"

Something about what Horatio had said tickled the back of his mind, and before the other man could even answer, he remembered — Oaker, the wagon-master, had been from there.

He interjected, "Was the town of Monk's Corner much affected by the battle?"

Horatio thought for a moment, and answered. "Not from what the doctor related to me, no. That accursed Colonel Tarleton led the British forces there, however, so there is no guessing what violences he might have taken it into his head to visit upon the unfortunate place where he found our detachment."

He continued, grimly, "No, the worst of it was that Tarleton was able to seize all of the horse and powder that the brigade had brought with them, in addition to chasing our men off into the swamps."

James' frown creased his face deeply. "So the enemy has

weakened our position here considerably, while at the same time strengthening their own. Is there any word of an evacuation?"

"Nay, not with the British in control of the harbor and the seas beyond. It's my understanding that this loss closes off the last opportunity to remove our forces from this town."

"So, it is to be a siege, then . . . but this time we are the ones holding the city against an attacking force."

Horatio nodded. He seemed about to add something else, but they were interrupted by a shout from one of the attendants, who hurried to be within earshot. "You fellows, come quick. Doctor needs you in the smallpox building."

James frowned his confusion to Horatio, who shrugged in answer. Together, they turned and began to make their slow way back to the isolated ward.

Alexandre stood at the doorway, clutching his hands together in obvious distress. James approached him and asked, "Whatever is the matter?"

The soldier answered in a burst of unintelligible French, and then shook his head angrily, repeating himself in English. "Sorry, I was too upset. Your friend Claude has been brought here to join you. It would appear that he had not actually had the pox before, but only claimed as much in order that he would be able to tend to you in your illness."

James sagged heavily onto his cane. "You mean to tell me that he is now afflicted?"

The French soldier nodded in sad agreement. "Aye, he has the fever and upon examining him, Doctor Ashford discovered that his skin was manifesting the first flush of the pox across his chest."

"Can I speak with him? Will you translate for me?"

"Of course," Alexandre answered, and followed James into the room.

On the next bed down from where Horatio had suffered his bout with the disease and recovered, Claude lay, looking gray and drawn, but he opened his eyes and sat up with a grim, determined expression when he saw James.

James said to Alexandre, "Have you asked him why he took the chance of becoming infected with the pox, when you and Doctor Ashford were wholly capable of caring for us?"

Alexandre shrugged. "Not yet, but I will." He spoke to Claude, relaying the question.

Claude answered, speaking not to his countryman, but directly to James, his eyes burning. "*Memoire . . . et revenge . . . et fraternité.*"

The effort of speaking these few words seemed to be enough to exhaust the French soldier, and his shoulders slumped as his eyes slid closed again.

Alexandre turned to James and asked quietly, "I take it you understood that well enough?"

James grimaced. "Oh, yes, well enough indeed."

Chapter 25

James looked at the court official, his rheumy eyes swelling with tears. "So you see, Legrand's bravery was found in the hospital, even more so than on the field of battle."

The official removed his glasses and folded them, setting them on the desk in front of him. James could see that the man was affected by the story, and could hear it in his voice when he asked, "Did Legrand . . . recover from the pox?"

James shook his head slowly. "Nay, he declined with shocking speed, and was gone even before the British took the town. Doctor Ashford said that he probably had an easier fate than did Alexandre, though."

The court official shot him a questioning look, and James said, "When they took us all prisoner, the British rounded up the men of the *Chasseurs-Volontaires*, free men in their own country, and sold them as slaves on Barbados."

James' chin dropped to his chest for a moment, and then he took a deep breath and looked up at the official. "I could forgive the British for cutting up my regiment at Savannah. I could forgive them even for fighting to maintain their hold on their American colonies. But what I can never forgive them for is taking those men, who served with dedication and bravery equal to any man on that battlefield, and selling them like animals to be worked to death on sugar plantations."

His mouth a grim line, he added, "Nor shall I rest until every man who is held in that evil institution of slavery has been returned to his birthright of freedom."

The court official paled at the sudden fierceness in the old man's tone. With a small quaver, he asked, "Certainly you aren't one of those abolitionists, then, in spite of the murders and uprisings up in Virginia?"

"Oh, yes, I certainly am," James said, without hesitation. "I'll have no part in such violence, but I cannot bring myself to condemn those who find no other alternative."

The court official fetched his glasses and polished them again before carefully putting them back on. "I see," was his only comment.

He looked over the statement he'd taken from James, his mouth pinched, as though this dull task had become suddenly distasteful. "Very well. You enlisted in 1779 under Captain Tolliver, completed your training, fought at the siege of Savannah, went on to Charleston, were took with the pox and were unable to fight in the siege of that city, then you were taken prisoner by the British and paroled as a Continental soldier, and returned home thereafter?"

James said, mildly, "That's true, though it leaves out most all of what I've told you."

The official made a small, dismissive gesture. "The Congress doesn't care beyond being able to establish that you have earned the pension." He fixed James with a look over the top of his glasses. "Though, I shouldn't be surprised if they were to suspend the pension paid to anyone who is convicted of a serious crime in this or any of the other states, so mind that your sense of duty to your battlefield companions does not drive you from the right side of the law."

James gave the man a sour look. "I have spent more than fifty years working to fulfill my oath to my brothers. I have remembered them every day of my life since that night with the rum, and I have done what I could to have my revenge against the British. In all that time, I have never committed a crime, petty or serious, and you think I need to be admonished *now?*"

He shook his head. "No, my opposition to slavery is a wholly separate thing from my oath, and I must hold on to the hope that our promise of life, liberty, and the pursuit of happiness may yet be honored for all men. I should be ashamed to have fought for a country that could do otherwise, after all, and so my zeal in working to bring about the end of slavery is the same as my pride at having served in the Revolution."

The official said nothing, but finished scratching down the conclusion of James' statement.

After a moment, he turned the paper around on the desk and offered the old man the pen. "Very well, then. Make your mark here, and I will witness it. Your service will be recorded, and in due course, I expect that your pension will be awarded. What you do with your time is your own affair, sir, but I take your meaning clearly enough."

James bent over the paper, carefully writing the letters of his name. His would not be the ignominious "X" of the illiterate, even if it paled in comparison to the graceful copperplate of the official's signature.

The official stood, offering his hand. "Thank you for your service, sir, and for letting me help you set it down in writing. I wish you success in your efforts, even if I do not fully understand your reasoning."

James took the man's hand as he stood. "I can ask no more of any man," he said. He left the courthouse, emerging into the dazzling afternoon light, and glanced southward. His mouth settled into a tight line, and he murmured to himself, "Memory . . . and revenge . . . and brotherhood."

Also in Audiobook

Many readers love the experience of turning the pages in a paper book such as the one you hold in your hands. Others enjoy hearing a skilled narrator tell them a story, bringing the words on the page to life.

Brief Candle Press has arranged to have *The Oath* produced as a high-quality audiobook, and you can listen to a sample and learn where to purchase it in that form by scanning the QR code below with your phone, tablet, or other device, or going to the Web address shown.

Happy listening!

tfar.us/TheOathAudio

Historical Notes

As usual, I have done my best to adhere to the history that can be known from the records — both official and unofficial — that survive from the incident that forms the heart of my story. Sadly, few official records remain of the *Chasseurs-Volontaires* of Saint-Domingue who came as part of the French force that tried — and failed — to retake Savannah, Georgia from the British in 1779.

After it achieved independence a couple of years later, Saint-Domingue took its modern name of Haiti, and its history since then has been plagued with misfortune, both man-made and natural.

Most salient to the work of writing a convincing story of those brave volunteers, the national archives burned, blew up, and burned again on no less than three separate occasions, meaning that most of what we have today to document their involvement at Savannah comes from reports and records of the American and mainland French forces they served amongst.

All of that said, I have knowingly played fast and loose with the historical record in a few places. I always figure it's better for me to "tell on myself" than to wait for a more rigorous historian to raise objections to my fiction on the grounds that it is unrealistic.

First of all, the sequence of events at the trenches in the days immediately following the American arrival was somewhat different from what I've depicted. In order to build up dramatic tension, I wrote a relatively slow escalation of encounters with the British, culminating in the feint which tricked the allies into firing on one another — which did happen, tragically — and then the disastrous ambush outside the trench under construction.

In fact, the major ambush — in which the French forces, and the *Chasseurs-Volontaires* specifically, suffered terrible casualties even before the disastrous assault on the British emplacements — took place *first,* making the confused intramural fighting even more horrifying.

While the ingredients of the rum oath were based on real oaths taken, particularly among the enslaved on Saint-Domingue, the details of the oath are largely of my own imagination. Under the circumstances that the characters were working, though, it made sense to me, and it certainly moved James' story forward in a compelling way.

The capture of a large British detachment — which records of the event claim consisted of anywhere from 111 to 140 men, plus two armed sloops and three merchant ships — by means of clever ruses at Colonel White's direction happened largely as described. My characters engage in some slight exaggerations, of course, but there is no doubt that it was a boost to the morale of the besiegers, and a blow to the defenders trapped within Savannah.

The aftermath of the battle on October 9, 1779 was every bit as awful as I've described, and though I hesitated to include the gruesome details of that afternoon, the fact that it marked the bloodiest single hour of the entire American War of Independence demanded that I honor the memories of those who lost their lives by declining to turn away from the carnage.

The story of Sergeant Jasper's exploits at the defense of

Fort Moultrie at Charles-Town makes a brief appearance in *The Declaration*, and, like my characters, I was surprised and saddened to learn of his demise in Savannah as I wrote this book. I thought that his gallantry and devotion to ensuring that the symbols that inspired and heartened the Americans fighting at both of these scenes of the American Revolution were worth mentioning.

Desertion from both the French and American forces was a constant issue in the days and weeks following the failure of the allied forces to retake Savannah, although I found no real evidence that the deserters were motivated by anything but the desire to exit the fight, having experienced some of the most horrifying battlefield scenes of the entire Revolution.

I have no evidence that there was a serious discussion about pressing into practical enslavement the men of the detachment of the *Chasseurs-Volontaires* who were sent from Savannah with the American forces to care for the wounded. However, I do know that one of the senior officers present at Charles-Town was Henry Laurens (yes, of *Hamilton* fame), who decried the failure of South-Carolina law to permit the raising of a Black regiment in that state in a letter to Washington. Had any proposal been raised to reduce to brute labor the detachment from Saint-Domingue, I trust that Laurens would have sprung up to quash it.

General Lincoln, the commander of the siege at Savannah and the defenses at Charleston, did complain bitterly in a letter to Washington about his inability to demand provision of slaves ("the only Labourers in this country") from the plantations in the area, so I have probably been too charitable in my depiction of his response to this imagined argument between his officers.

Given that at this writing, we are well into the second year of a global pandemic, it is only surprising that it took this long for smallpox to make a substantial appearance in one of my stories. The smallpox epidemic that raged across North America at the time of the Revolution was a larger military factor earlier in the war, particularly during the Northern Campaign of 1776, until General Washington's now-familiar and highly controversial decision to order inoculation for all Continental troops.

Unlike modern vaccination, which stimulates an immune response by presenting the body's immune system with some inert or greatly weakened element of the infectious agent, smallpox inoculation involved introducing a sample from an infected person into a small cut in a healthy person's skin — infecting them with the full-strength smallpox virus, but in a manner that — for reasons still poorly understood — did not manifest as the full-blown disease . . . usually.

Because of small risk of contracting the disease itself, and the more serious risk of transmitting it to others while recovering from the inoculation, the general's order was opposed by many, but it succeeded in reducing the smallpox epidemic as a factor in the military calculations as he tried to counter British moves across the entire eastern seaboard and beyond.

That is not to say that there weren't outbreaks from time to time, however, and as depicted, not all militia units adopted the Continental Army's inoculation practices, leaving their soldiers vulnerable if they did come into contact with the dread disease. In healthy patients, smallpox would kill between one in ten and one in three. However, as with any grave illness, those who came into their fight with the smallpox virus already weakened by wounds or other diseases fared much worse.

It is a cruel irony of history that the same men who lost so much at the walls of Savannah were immediately tasked with the doomed defense of Charles-Town. Having undertaken siege warfare from the offensive side, they then had to endure it in the role of defenders.

The terrain around Savannah gave the advantage to the British, as did the quality of their leadership, compared to the leadership of the allies. At Charles-Town, the advantages of terrain were reversed, as the British were able to take possession of the high ground to the west of the town, and use that commanding location to lob cannonballs — and, by the end of the siege, superheated "hot shots" — into the city, leading to the outbreak of fires.

Further moves cut off supply lines from overland and by water, so the American position in the city was impossible to maintain. The surrender of the force at Charles-Town was one of the most severe outright defeats that the American side suffered over the entire course of the war.

I found it relatively easy to conceive that the close contact between American soldiers and the gallant *Chasseurs-Volontaires* would have left some of the Americans deeply aware of the humanity of the enslaved Blacks who labored in bondage, even as the new nation congratulated itself on having established liberty for its citizens.

I don't think it's a great leap, then to think that some of these soldiers would have gone on to take part in the burgeoning abolition movement in the early part of the 19th century. While I don't have direct evidence of any of the veterans of the Revolution claiming their pensions for the express purpose of devoting the proceeds to the movement to end slavery, it's almost impossible to imagine that none did so.

Those pension records, though, are a rich source of research material both for historians and fictionalizers of the Revolution. Because they were required in order to claim pension benefits, and had to be presented as accurate under oath, they are some of the most detailed and reliable firsthand reports that we have of the experiences of ordinary soldiers.

Acknowledgements

Much of my research is conducted entirely online, drawing on the riches of correspondence, journals, military reports, and so forth that have been digitized in our marvelous modern era.

This time, I was able to spend time on the ground in some of the settings of my story, and while I wound up telling a different tale than I'd anticipated exploring for Georgia, this book is immeasurably better for my having been able to see the state for myself.

I am happy to acknowledge my friend Jeff Clarke, who graciously hosted me at his home, permitted me to experience firing a musket for the first time, and brought me to (among other places) the quiet and isolated site of the Battle of Kettle Creek.

That place had been recently studied and found to have had the traces of the mortal remains of soldiers who fell there, scattered across the back of the strategic hill that helped to shape the outcome. It was deeply moving to be there, in the very place, and it seemed better preserved to its original state than are many of the sites of the Revolution.

While I regret that the stories those bones wanted to tell was not the one that I ended up telling here, the experience did inform and improve this story, as well, and I am forever grateful to Jeff for that opportunity.

My devoted editor, Jen McDonnell, again helped to ensure that this is a better book than it might otherwise have been. Her corrections and suggestions ensured that it reads more smoothly, and more fully tells the story of those men from Saint-Domingue, and the Americans who came to know and respect them.

Thank You

I deeply appreciate you spending the past couple of hundred pages with the characters and events of a world long past, yet hopefully relevant today.

If you enjoyed this book, I'd also be grateful for a kind review on your favorite bookseller's Web site or social media outlet. Word of mouth is the best way to make me successful, so that I can bring you even more high-quality stories of bygone times.

To hear about my newest releases, appearances, special offers, and more, sign up for my monthly newsletter at https://tfar.us/newsletter.

I'd love to hear directly from you, too — feel free to reach out to me via my Facebook page, Twitter feed, or Web site and let me know what you liked, and what you would like me to work on more.

Again, thank you for reading, for telling your friends about this book, for giving it as a gift or dropping off a copy in your favorite classroom or library. With your support and encouragement, we'll find even more times and places to explore together.

larsdhhedbor.com
Facebook: Lars.D.H.Hedbor
@LarsDHHedbor on Twitter

Enjoy a preview of the next book in the
Tales From a Revolution series:

<u>*The Powder*</u>

For countless centuries, the surf had rolled in on this beach, with the steady rhythm of calm seas like tonight's, or the wilder crash and ebb of a storm. It would continue doing so for countless eons after his name was forgotten, the sea taking no note that anyone named Harold Cooper had ever existed.

Tonight, though, something was different, and it had every nerve in his body on alert. Even though he knew intellectually that he should not be able to sense it, he was aware that somewhere out there beyond the surf, an American ship lurked in the darkness, its presence a rebuke to Royal authority on the island of Bermuda.

Harold — Hal to his friends, and 'that accursed rascal' to his enemies — had but a small part to play in this night's plans, but he could not help but think that it might secure his place in the annals of the island's history, if ever it could be spoken of.

At the moment, though, the only thing demanded of him was that he wait, and hope. He peered into the darkness, but could discern nothing other than the stars slowly wheeling through the sky into the inky murmuring darkness of the Atlantic Ocean, the moon glinting off an occasional wave in the distance.

He reflected on the strange and discomforting road that had led him to this desperate action, which was technically an act of treason against the Crown. He supposed that it had all started with Molly.

"What do you mean, that you wouldn't consider accompanying me to the dance unless I were the last man on the entire island?"

Molly Haskins crossed her arms in front of herself and answered starchily, "Just what I said, Harold. You've failed in your apprenticeship to your father's business, and instead you've found nothing better than working on the docks as hard as a slave might, and moreover, you've a reputation as a rake among my friends."

Hal bristled. "I'll have you know that my work on the docks demands as much skill as did my father's business — and quite a lot less time under the lash than either my father or a foreman might apply. As for my reputation" — Hal grinned — "I'm no rake, but neither am I so unworldly that will I step on your foot as we dance, or slobber on your hand. I rather like to think of myself as refined than some alleyway hound."

Molly favored him with a dubious grimace. "In any event, with the trade being stopped by the Continental Congress in answer to Parliament's blockades of their harbors, what honest work can you even find on the docks?"

Hal had to admit that this was an awkward question to answer. At present there were no ships carrying food and supplies from the mainland colonies, and accepting what goods the islands could produce. As a result, there had been distressingly little legitimate work of late for anyone on the docks, never mind for a barely-skilled stevedore.

After a long pause, he considered the girl and said quietly, "There is always some traffic, even if it is from sources that Parliament neither knows nor approves of."

Molly's frown deepened. "You are hardly improving your standing, Harold, by hinting that you might be involved in smuggling."

Hal made a shushing motion with his hands and hissed, "Not so loud, Molly." Then he shrugged, adding, "When the law makes it impossible to fill our bellies legally, haven't we an obligation to break the law?"

Her expression grew thoughtful as she considered his argument for a moment. Finally, she said, "It depends upon the nature of the law. If you must deny somebody else their bread in order for you to eat, it seems difficult to justify that exchange. However, if you are defying a distant and wrathful body of men who seek only to exact revenge upon the people of a town far from here, and are well-satisfied to injure us by incident . . . I suppose I could see that obligation."

She pursed her lips, though, adding, "Not that it makes any difference whether you hang from a gibbet for stealing from a neighbor or for cheating the Parliament of their claimed due. Your pitiable remains will be of no use to me or anyone, whatever brought them there."

Look for The Powder: Tales From a Revolution - Bermuda *at your favorite booksellers.*